TROUBLE IN
ZOMBIE-TOWN

Also by Mark Cheverton

Invasion of the Overworld
Battle for the Nether
Confronting the Dragon

Jungle Temple Oracle
Last Stand on the Ocean Shore

Saving Crafter

MARK CHEVERTON

TROUBLE IN ZOMBIE-TOWN

A GAMEKNIGHT999 ADVENTURE

SIMON AND SCHUSTER

First published in Great Britain in 2015
by Simon & Schuster UK Ltd
A CBS company
Originally published in the USA in 2014 by Sky Pony Press

10 9 8 7 6 5 4 3 2 1

Simon & Schuster UK Ltd
1st Floor, 222 Gray's Inn Road
London WC1X 8HB

A CIP catalogue record for this book is available from the British Library

PB ISBN: 978-1-4711-5848-3
Ebook ISBN: 978-1-4711-4436-3

Printed and bound by CPI Group (UK) Ltd, Croydon, CR0 4YY

www.simonandschuster.co.uk

Siblings are the best friends that you take for granted when you are young, and treasure when you are old.

CHAPTER 1

THE VILLAIN

He materialized onto the lush green blocky landscape with a hateful sneer on his blocky face, his whole being filled with a destructive loathing for the natural beauty that surrounded him. Walking toward a nearby sheep, he grinned as the square fluffy creature bolted away across the blocky hill, a look of terror in its soft square eyes. An evil presence seemed to emanate from him like the heat from a burning house. Even blades of grass wanted to lean away from this sinister creature.

"How can these Overworlders tolerate this place?" the dark creature hissed as he glared at his surroundings.

In the distance, he could see a village, this one not fortified like many were these days. It was the normal collection of houses, each made from individual blocks, as all things were in Minecraft, formed from many cubes of wood. The squat structures were clustered around a central stone building that stretched high up into the air: the watchtower. Nearby, he could see the village well and a field of wheat growing in the distance. Lurking in the alleyways between the buildings, he could see the villagers going about their work, their boxy heads and long rectangular bodies almost blending in with the blocky homes.

These foolish villagers are oblivious to the danger they're in, the sinister creature thought to himself. He would soon correct their mistake.

Closing his glowing white eyes, he teleported away from the scenic view and materialized in a dark shadowy tunnel. Drawing in a full breath, he let out an abrasive guttural wail that echoed throughout the stone passages and rocky chambers, bouncing off lava pools and reflecting from towering waterfalls until it filled the underground world of Minecraft. In an instant, his call was greeted by the sorrowful wails of zombies.

"I am coming, my children," he yelled to the darkness. "Prepare a Gathering."

The wails changed from sounds of despair and sadness to those of surprise and fear. The dark stranger smiled; he could feel their fear . . . good.

Moving silently through the dark passages, he descended through the tunnels, heading for that secret entrance that only the monsters of the night knew existed. Occasionally he saw giant spiders and creepers hiding in the shadows, hoping to avoid being seen, but none escaped his glowing eyes. He saw them all, their cowering forms veiled in darkness. Normally, these fearful creatures would have been destroyed, for their fear disgusted him, but he had far more important plans to worry about, and didn't have time for these weaklings.

A glow started to fill the tunnel ahead, the soft

orange illumination of lava, warm inviting lava. The shadows behind stone pillars and deep crevasses began to grow dark and long as he neared the source of the light. As he turned a corner, he was greeted by a long flow of molten stone that spilled down from high above, forming a broad pool. Nearby, a waterfall gurgled its cool waters from a hole in the wall, the long blue stream flowing into the boiling pool. Where the opposites met, obsidian was formed, the black speckled blocks reflecting the light from the molten stone and casting beams of light throughout the chamber.

This was it.

The entrance to Zombie-town was always near the meeting of water and lava. Casting his glowing gaze across the jagged stone walls, he instantly saw the pattern that masked the secret door: a flat section of stone with a single block sticking out. Moving to the outlier, he placed his hand against the block and pressed. A click sounded, then the wall swung inward revealing a long dark tunnel. Stepping into the passage, the stranger turned and closed the stone door, then sprinted down the rocky corridor. As he ran, he could see the end of the path growing brighter, the walls changing from the stone grey to an inviting orange, like the coming of autumn. More lava: the stranger smiled an eerie smile. He loved lava . . . it always reminded him of home.

When he reached the end of the tunnel, he stopped and looked at his surroundings. Before him stood a massive chamber that stretched upward maybe twenty blocks or more, and at least a hundred blocks across. All across the chamber floor were small homes built out of stone and dirt, each a different size and shape. The blocky structures seemed to be competing with each other, walls pushing against walls in a battle for space that seemed to create a patchwork of geometry that had a strange kind of chaotic beauty to it. Nothing matched, nothing was the same, and yet every Zombie-town looked like every other.

A large clearing could be seen positioned at the center of the chamber, the encroaching buildings kept away by some kind of mystical force. That was his destination. Taking the blocky steps two at a time, the dark stranger ran down to the cavern floor then sprinted through the maze of narrow streets, turning this way and that in a confused serpentine path that wended its way through the town. At some points, he found the walkway blocked by the corners of houses. Drawing his diamond pick, he quickly smashed through the blocks, leaving the damage behind as he streaked for the clearing.

In minutes, he'd traversed the floor of the cavern and reached the edge of the clearing. Near the edge of the open square, strange green sparks seemed to shoot up into an air like the fireworks for some kind of alien celebration. Zombies stood around these sparkling fountains, just standing beneath them, bathing in their flow, their dark eyes closed in blissful contentment. The stranger knew that these were the HP fountains that zombies depended on for life. They did not eat 'brains' as the foolish users thought; that was a silly myth. Zombies fed by standing within the emerald flow of the HP fountains, the green sparks restoring their health and sating their hunger. He knew that if a zombie spent too much time away from a zombie-town, then they would die. As a result, they were forced to always stay nearby, shackled to their underground existence forever.

Zooming past these zombies, the stranger headed for the stone dais that stood at the center of the clearing. Pushing through the crowd of monsters, he saw zombies of every size and age, large, small, the young and the old. He also saw zombie-pigmen and the occasional blaze, likely visiting from the Nether by using the secret portals that connected them. When he reached the steps leading up to the raised platform, he let out another abrasive guttural wail. This drew everyone's attention.

Slowly, he walked up the steps. Another zombie was on the stage, this creature muscular and strong; he was likely the leader of the community . . . but not for long. The stranger moved to the zombie's side and glared up at him with his glowing eyes.

"What is your name?" the dark stranger asked.

"This zombie is called Va-Lok," he said in a scratchy animal-like voice, pointing to himself with a stubby green finger. "Va-Lok is the leader of this town."

"Not anymore."

The stranger attacked the zombie with a flurry of punches, raining damage down on the zombie. The creature tried to fight back, but his attacker was able to disappear just as the zombie claws were about to touch his skin. The stranger would then reappear behind Va-Lok and attack his exposed back, bringing him to the brink of death. This lasted for only a minute, the stranger attacking, disappearing, reappearing, attacking again . . . over and over. Va-Lok didn't stand a chance. When only the smallest trickle of health remained, the stranger shoved the zombie off the stage, causing him to fall to the ground. Landing hard, the damage from the fall erased the last of his XP. The creature disappeared, leaving behind pieces of zombie flesh and three glowing balls of XP. They drifted to those nearest the victim.

All eyes then shifted to the stranger.

"I have defeated your leader in combat and now claim this town as my own. This was done as it has always been done, the strong eliminating the weak, as it is written in your laws. You are all my subjects and will do as I command."

"What orders are given to the zombies of this town?" said one of the nearest zombies.

"What is your name?"

"This zombie is called Ta-Zin," he said as he stepped forward, a look of uncertainty and fear on his decaying face.

"Ta-Zin, you are now one of my generals. You will lead this town in battle," the stranger said in a loud voice that echoed off the walls of the chamber, making it sound as if there were a hundred of him. "You are to attack the Overworlders and continue to attack until the User-that-is-not-a-user comes before me on his knees." He paused to let his command sink in, then continued. "The first war which was to set us free failed. The idiotic leaders, Erebus and Malacoda, failed me, and their punishment was death. Now I will lead the Last Battle and show the pathetic NPCs of the Overworld what fear really is."

The zombies started to murmur to each other, their rotting heads nodding up and down, toothy smiles showing on green, boxy faces.

"We will attack the villagers until the User-that-is-not-a-user comes before me and kneels, begging for the lives of these pitiful NPCs. And when he is near death, when the last bit of his health is about to evaporate, his courage will shatter, and this Gameknight999 will take the Gateway of Light back to the physical world to escape his death. And when he does that, I will ride the Gateway with him into the physical world where I will be free to cause havoc and punish mankind for my imprisonment within Minecraft. Then and only then will I be able to free the monsters of the night."

The zombies shouted out a guttural cheer that

sounded more like a growl than an exclamation, but then grew silent as Ta-Zin stepped forward. The zombie turned to look at the crowd of monsters behind him, bringing all their cold dead eyes to him, then gazed up at the stranger.

"This zombie is confused. It can be seen by the clothes being worn that the leader standing before zombie-town is a shadow-crafter, one of the ancient ones that can change those that live in the shadows, make improvements to the creatures of the night, but . . ."

The stranger teleported to the zombie's side and pummeled him with punches, his fists a blur, reducing the monster's HP to nearly zero, but then the attack stopped just as Ta-Zin fell to one knee.

"I am not *a* shadow-crafter, I am *THE* shadow-crafter," the stranger said, his voice filled with rage. "I *created* the shadow-crafters and am the ruler of all the creatures of Minecraft."

"Ta-Zin apologizes," Ta-Zin said with a strained voice. "How should the zombies address their new leader?" As the zombies knew, all non-monsters were named for their task, their purpose within Minecraft. A shadow-crafter that improved zombies would be called Zombiebrine, one that crafted creepers would be called Creeperbrine . . . "What thing does the leader craft?"

"I am the crafter of creatures like the failed Erebus and the overzealous Malacoda. I create the leaders of armies and the rulers of darkness. I CRAFT EVIL HEROES!" His voice echoed off the chamber walls like a hammer to a gong. "Now go forth and destroy, and tell the NPCs they will suffer until the cowardly User-that-is-not-a-user decides to face me!"

"But what is the leader's name?" a zombie yelled from the crowd. "How should the leader of zombie-town be addressed?"

"My name . . . you want to know my name?"

Ta-Zin nodded his sickly green head. The stranger leaned in close, and his voice was a spine-tingling whisper.

"You call me as the legends have named me . . . I am Herobrine."

CHAPTER 2
NEW BEGINNINGS

ameknight999 logged into Minecraft like he always had a thousand times before. He was playing in his basement, using his father's high-powered computer, the one with the advanced graphics that made the game run really fast. Looking over his shoulder, he could see his father's inventions all over the basement: the 3D licorice printer, the marshmallow launcher, the high-speed peanut butter mixer . . . inventions of all kinds. That's what his father's job was: being an inventor. He created the most unusual things, then traveled all over the country trying to sell them to anyone that might buy them. Most of his creations were failures, few if any actually working as expected, with the exception of one: the digitizer. Gameknight had learned the hard way that this one actually functioned better than expected, as it had digitized him and pulled him into the program that had been running on the computer: Minecraft. It had been a painful lesson that he would never repeat.

He could still remember his initial terror at being sucked into the game . . . that gigantic spider he had to battle . . . and the zombies . . . and the creepers . . . and the . . . The monsters seemed to go on forever. Gameknight hadn't turned on the digitizer on purpose; it had been an accident. But that little accident had propelled him on an adventure that changed his life forever. Many things had been learned on his journey through Minecraft, but the most startling had been that the creatures within the game were actually alive . . . the NPCs and the animals . . . *and* the monsters . . .

Two evil beings in particular had made it their jobs to terrify Gameknight999 and threaten all the lives within Minecraft: Erebus, the king of the endermen, and Malacoda, the king of the Nether. Both had made it their mission to destroy Minecraft by destroying the Source. This was where all software came from to run all of the Minecraft world servers. If they destroyed the Source, then they could have escaped into the physical world. But Gameknight999, with the help of his friends and an army of NPCs and users, had stopped Erebus and Malacoda and saved everyone. It had been a great experience that had taught him much about himself, but also had changed how he viewed Minecraft, forever. Once he was inside, it was no longer just a game for Gameknight999 . . . it was so much more.

Looking over his shoulder, he could see the digitizer sitting there amidst the clutter of the basement, its pointed ray gun-looking frame aimed at the basement wall. It just sat there, turned off, its tubes looking dark and ominous. That device gave him the chills whenever he looked at it. But now, a few weeks after escaping from the game and miraculously staying alive, he finally had the courage to come back down into the basement and play his favorite game again . . . Minecraft.

Turning back to his large 1080p monitor, he saw his character materialized in the normal area just outside the hidey-hole that he'd built when he'd been pulled into Minecraft by the digitizer. Looking up, he couldn't see the server thread that connected his character to the Minecraft servers (and to the Source), but Gameknight knew that it was there. That was how the NPCs could distinguish a user from an NPC: the server thread that stretched up into the sky like a silvery beam of light. They could also see the letters of the user's name floating above the user's head. When he'd been pulled into Minecraft he looked like a user, with his moniker floating above his head, but the shining server thread was absent. He was a user, but without the connection to the servers . . . he was also not one. The NPCs called him the User-that-is-not-a-user, the one prophesized to save Minecraft, and he had taken that title with pride.

Now his character was looking out across the landscape. Gameknight could see the tall rocky outcropping that extended over the basin, a long stream of water falling from its heights and splashing into the underground chamber. That was where he'd first been attacked by the giant spider. The waterfall had saved his life that day. He could still remember every detail of the terrifying creature, the little hairs all over its body that seemed to move on their own; those wicked black curved claws at the end of each leg; the multitude of eyes all burning with a hatred that was insatiable. The memory made him shiver slightly, but he knew that it was different now. He had been in the game, really *in* the game. But now, he was just playing it; a normal user out for a stroll in Minecraft. His character might take damage, might even get killed, but nothing would happen to him in real life. This was just a harmless computer game and it was going to stay that way. Besides, there was nothing in this world that could make him take the Gateway of Light (his father's digitizer) back into Minecraft: never again.

Looking back at the screen, Gameknight999 moved his character out of the basin and toward the village that he knew was in the distance. He sprinted across the landscape, moving past another mountain with a similar rocky outcropping. This one had long columns of stone hanging down from the overhanging surface that looked like giant fangs of some kind of ancient blocky leviathan. He remembered this mountain from the first time on this server, and it had scared him back then . . . but everything had scared him back then.

Streaking past the rocky peak, he sprinted straight toward Crafter's village. A few spiders came out to challenge him, but Gameknight left them alone. He knew that with his enchanted armor and sword, these spiders did not stand a chance against him, and besides . . . they were alive and he didn't want to fight them, or kill them, if it wasn't necessary.

That was one of the things that he'd learned after being pulled into the game by his father's digitizer; the creatures within the game were really alive. The villagers, or NPCs (non-playable characters) had hopes and dreams for their children and felt sadness and despair when they lost a loved one. All of the creatures within the digital realms felt pain and feared death; they were sentient and knew that they existed, and now Gameknight carried that knowledge with him as well.

Running past the eight-legged monsters, he nodded at them, acknowledging them but veering around them as he continued on toward the village. After a few minutes, he could start to see the tall cobblestone wall that they'd erected around the village. It was built to protect the NPCs from the monsters of the Overworld that had been led by the king of the endermen, Erebus.

Erebus had led the assault on Minecraft in an attempt to get to the Source. If they had been successful, they could have destroyed the Source and killed all of the digital lives that existed within Minecraft. Then they could have taken the Gateway of Light to the physical world where they would have wreaked havoc and destroyed everything. Gameknight and his friends in the village ahead had led the defense of Minecraft and saved everyone. And now, thankfully, there were no battles, no monsters seeking his death, no armies clashing on the battlefield. There was just Minecraft . . . and that's how he liked it.

As he approached the village, he could see an NPC standing atop a tall stone tower that loomed over all the buildings. That was the watchtower and every village had one. The NPC with the best eyesight would be assigned the task of watching for monsters. They would be named Watcher, for NPCs are named after their task, e.g., Builder, Runner, Planter, Digger . . . It always reassured Gameknight when he saw Watchers in their position atop the towers. That meant that things were as they should be. But this time, there were two Watchers . . . strange.

"Open the gates," one of the Watchers yelled.

Two iron doors swung open as Gameknight approached, but as they creaked open, he thought he saw deep scratches carved into the surface as if four razor-sharp claws and been dragged across their cold iron surface. Looking up, he could see archers walking the battlements atop the wall, each with their bow in their hands, arrow notched.

Why would there be so many archers up on the walls today? Gameknight thought.

Crossing the wooden bridge that spanned the encircling moat, Gameknight moved into the central square. He was hailed by every NPC that saw him. They all knew him, of course; he was the savior of Minecraft . . . the User-that-is-not-a-user.

As he moved into the village, two young NPCs ran toward him, huge smiles painted across their faces.

"Gameknight!!!" they yelled as they sprinted to him.

Kneeling to the ground, Gameknight999 held his arms out as they dived into him. Scooping them up, he held them close to his chest as he spun around, their little legs dangling outward like seats on some kind of rotating carnival ride, their giggles filling the air. Stopping the ride, he slowly settled them to the ground and released his grip, letting the twins run off on some new childish adventure.

They were Topper and Filler, the twin children of his NPC friend, Digger. They had adopted Gameknight999 and made him part of their family after he'd saved Minecraft. This humbled him, for he'd caused the death of Digger's wife, the twins' mother, back when he'd been a selfish griefer. Before he knew the great secret of Minecraft, that the NPCs were actually alive, Gameknight had done terrible things. When he first came to this village, back before the war that had assaulted all the servers, back before he'd become the User-that-is-not-a-user, Gameknight had griefed this village. He'd broken open doors to let zombies get to the villagers, and had smashed open walls to let the skeletons shoot their arrows at the inhabitants; that's what had caused the death of Digger's wife. After the great battle that had crashed down upon this village . . . after Gameknight had helped to fortify the village with the help of his user friend, Shawny . . . after he'd saved the lives of countless NPCs, Digger had come to forgive him for his past transgressions. This had always humbled him, and made Gameknight999 want to work hard to be deserving of this kindness, and Digger's twins, Topper and Filler, always reminded him of the incredible value of this gift with their warm hugs and joyous giggles.

The only thing that made him sad now was that he couldn't actually feel the hugs. He was just playing the game, watching on his computer monitor, hearing the voices of his NPC friends through his headset . . . he was just an observer and not part of the world that he was watching. He missed feeling those hugs, but he would never go back into the game for real, and become the User-that-is-not-a-user. It had nearly cost him his life and had been the most terrifying thing he'd ever experienced. No, he missed feeling the twins' warm embrace, but the cost to feel those loving arms was too great.

"Gameknight!" another young voice yelled.

Turning toward the sound, he saw a young girl running toward him. She had long curly red hair, but it was not flowing behind her as she ran, it was just stuck to her shoulders and back as if painted to her skin. It was Stitcher.

As just a regular user, things within Minecraft seemed so flat and two-dimensional. But when he'd been *in* the game, he could actually see Stitcher's long red curls flowing down her shoulders, bouncing like so many crimson springs as she ran. There were so many wonderful details in the world of Minecraft that normal users just couldn't see, details that made all the creatures look different and unique, and proved that the NPCs and animals and monsters inside the game really were alive!

She ran across the square and dove into him, dropping her bow and arrow as she flew through the air. He caught her easily, but the force of her momentum knocked him to the ground, laughing.

"You've gotten bigger since the last time I saw you," Gameknight said as he stood up.

"It has been a while since you've been here," she replied.

"Only a couple of weeks," Gameknight999 replied. He had to take a break after his last harrowing adventure.

She looked at him and frowned as if he were lying. Then he remembered time within Minecraft went faster than it did in the physical world; one day in Minecraft was only twenty minutes in the physical world.

"Yeah, I guess it has been longer than that," he said. "Sorry, I should have come back sooner."

"You're right, you should have," Stitcher replied, then punched him in the arm. "Next time, I'll punch you harder if you wait this long to come back and see us. We're your Minecraft family and don't you forget it!"

"Sorry," he said meekly.

A laugh came from behind. Spinning, he saw Hunter approaching, Stitcher's older sister. As always, she had her enchanted bow in her hand, and arrow notched, ready.

"Did my little sister just beat you up and put you in your place?" she asked.

"Yeah, kinda," Gameknight replied.

Hunter laughed even louder. She too looked as if she'd aged. Her flowing red hair was longer, the strands reaching down to the center of her back, but painted flat. It took something away from her appearance, as if she were just one of the multitudes instead of someone unique. She also looked taller, now as tall as Gameknight. Much about her had changed, but not her eyes. Her deep brown eyes still showed the fury and anger she felt toward the monsters that had killed her parents and destroyed her village. Gameknight could see that her thirst for revenge still filled her being, and this made him sad, for revenge is a hungry master that consumes both the prey and the predator. His mother always said the best revenge was to live life fully, to be successful, and to be happy. But Gameknight could tell that Hunter was not ready to hear this . . . not yet.

"Well, if you're done having my little sister beat you up, we have much to discuss," Hunter explained. "Come, to the crafting chamber."

She spun gracefully on one foot and headed for the center of the village, toward the tall stone tower that stood like a sentinel, watching over the inhabitants. Gameknight followed behind, Stitcher at his side.

Many cheered as they saw Gameknight pass by; he'd saved all of their lives and was a hero . . . no, a legend, a living legend: the User-that-is-not-a-user, the one that stopped the monsters of Minecraft from destroying everything and everyone. Villager after villager shouted out his name and patted him on the back as he ran through the village. It made Gameknight feel good about himself, something that he was not used to feeling; like he was someone important, someone valuable and worthwhile. He didn't normally feel this way at home, and especially at school. In middle school, Gameknight999 was just Tommy Feynman, the kid that tried to be invisible, because that was how you easily avoided bullies. He didn't feel important or significant or valuable, because feeling like that was how you attracted the bullies, by standing tall and standing out. No, school was not where he excelled; Minecraft was where he did that. And now that he had friends here, in Minecraft, he could feel good about himself at last.

When they reached the tall cobblestone tower, Hunter opened the door and moved to the far corner of the room. Glancing up the ladder, Gameknight could see archers on the various floors, each with arrow notched, looking out the window as if expecting some kind of attack.

What was going on here? he thought.

Drawing her diamond pickaxe, she swung it at the corner block, shattering it with three swings, exposing the secret tunnel that was hidden in every watchtower; it was the entrance to the subterranean crafting chamber that sat beneath every village. Tossing the block aside, she dropped down into the tunnel with practiced ease. Stitcher then followed right behind, her petite form disappearing from sight. Gameknight was about to follow them, but first glanced up the ladder to the upper floors. The archers looked anxious. *Why would they be so nervous?*

Stitcher's red hair suddenly popped up out of the shaft, her brown eyes looking up at Gameknight999, a confused look on her face.

"You coming or just gonna do some sightseeing for a while?" She smiled.

"Yeah, I'm coming."

She disappeared down the dark tunnel, then Gameknight stepped down onto the ladder. He slid down a few rungs then stopped and looked up at the bright opening. Questions rolled through his head like a thunderstorm.

Something is going on . . . something unexpected. I don't like unexpected.

Shaking that familiar feeling that something bad

was about to happen, he slid down the ladder into the shadowy depths of Minecraft.

CHAPTER 3

THE SMALLEST RIPPLE

A s Gameknight slid down to the bottom of the ladder, questions bounced around in his head. *What was going on? Why did everyone seem on edge? Why all the warriors on the wall?* The questions burst through his head like bolts of lighting, each one flashing brighter than the last across his mental landscape. A few times, he had to stop and consider certain ideas, his mind focused so tightly on the questions that he thought he might fall from the ladder.

When he finally made it to the bottom of the ladder, he found Hunter and Stitcher impatiently waiting for him, an agitated look on Hunter's face.

"What took you so long?" Hunter asked.

"Ahh . . . I was just thinking," Gameknight answered. "I mean . . . what's with all the archers? There were two Watchers and a bunch of archers in the tower. And I noticed there were lots of soldiers on the walls. It looks like you're getting ready for an attack. What's going on?"

"You need to talk about it with Crafter," Hunter answered. "All I know is, the war isn't over yet, and the zombie problem still needs to be taken care of."

"The zombie problem?" Gameknight asked.

"Yeah, you know . . . They need to be taken care of . . . if you know what I mean."

"Why, have they attacked your village?" Gameknight asked.

"They have before and they will again!" Hunter said. "And we've got to get rid of them before they do." Pausing to take a breath, Hunter turned to her sister. "The monsters destroyed our village, abducted you, and killed our parents and all our friends. They destroyed everything. Zombies can never be trusted!"

She paused for a moment, and Gameknight could see the pain on her face grow as she relived the destruction of their village. Her eyes grew angrier and angrier as the memories flooded through her mind.

"They are monsters and we are NPCs," Hunter growled. "There will never be peace between our two races, and the only way this war will end is when one of us is wiped out, and I vote it's them and not us. Any objections?"

Nobody said anything. They just let Hunter's anger slowly dissipate.

"I didn't see any zombies out and about," Gameknight said. "Are you sure they're coming to attack the village?"

"Of course they're coming," Hunter said. "It's what zombies do, attack, then attack again and again. It's the only thing they know how to do, other than moan and growl."

"But I thought the war was over," Gameknight said. "We beat Malacoda and Erebus and saved the Source. I figured the fighting would be over."

"I don't know if it can ever be over," Hunter added. "Our history with the monsters of Minecraft is based on fighting. When our hands were linked across our chests, before you freed them, we couldn't fight back, we were just victims waiting to get pounced. Now, the NPCs refuse to be the victims anymore."

"But it doesn't seem like there will ever be peace,"

Gameknight replied.

"That's right," Stitcher added, "Maybe we need to solve our problems by talking, not fighting."

Gameknight contemplated Stitcher's last remark, but said nothing. He wasn't sure how they could ever make peace with zombies . . . but maybe she was right . . . maybe they should try.

They traversed the torch-lit tunnel in silence. Gameknight remembered the many battles they'd had in tunnels like these while they moved across the server, staying just a few steps ahead of Malacoda's army of Nether-monsters. Peering deep into the shadowy tunnel, he half expected zombie claws to reach out at him at any instant. But he knew, deep down, that this tunnel was safe and those days of constant fighting and overwhelming fear were long past.

In minutes, they reached the end of the tunnel and entered the large circular chamber where he'd first met Crafter. It was empty save for a wooden table and chair at the center. At the far end of the chamber, Gameknight could see two iron doors, torches placed above each: the entrance to the crafting chamber. Moving to the metal doors, Hunter pounded on them with her blocky fist. Seconds later, an armored face peered through the inset windows. The guard looked at each of them, then glanced at the rest of the chamber, making sure there were no threats. Satisfied that all was safe, he pushed the button on their side of the door, causing it to swing open.

Why are they being so cautious? Gameknight thought. *What is it that has them so afraid?*

The trio entered the crafting chamber, and their ears were instantly assaulted by the cacophony of hammers ringing on metal, minecarts clattering across slatted tracks, and thirty NPCs crafting the tools of war. Gameknight was shocked by the activity. He hadn't seen a crafting chamber this busy since they had been preparing for the war to save Minecraft.

Moving down the steps that led to the floor of the chamber, Gameknight saw his best friend in Minecraft, Crafter, at the center of the maelstrom. He was moving from crafting bench to crafting bench, inspecting each NPC's work, commenting on the sharpness of a sword or the fletching of an arrow.

"CRAFTER!" Hunter shouted above the din.

The young boy turned toward the sound. His blue eyes glanced at Hunter, but then moved up to Gameknight. He smiled and dropped the arrow that he was inspecting into a nearby minecart, then ran to the foot of the stairs, his black smock swaying as he wended his way around the multitude of crafting benches. Leaping over an incoming minecart, he landed gracefully right in front of the trio.

"A rather dramatic entrance," Stitcher said with a mischievous smile.

Crafter shrugged and sped past her, then stopped in front of Gameknight999.

"Hello friend, it's good to see you again," Crafter said.

"Yeah, I think it's been a while, maybe a few weeks," Gameknight answered.

"A few weeks?" Hunter laughed.

Then Gameknight looked down at Crafter and noticed that his friend was a few inches taller, his face and body more mature. It looked as if he'd aged a couple of years instead of a couple of weeks. He had played Minecraft on and off over the last couple of weeks, but had steered clear of Crafter's server; the memories from the past adventures . . . battles with creatures of the Overworld and the monsters of the Nether, had still been fresh in his mind. Instead of looking for adventure within the digital realms, he'd instead been experimenting with making mods, the most recent his greatest creation.

"Ahh . . . sorry I've been away for so long," Gameknight stammered, feeling bad for his absence, "but I'm back now."

"Well, you are a welcome sight Gameknight999," Crafter said, putting a blocky hand on his friend's shoulder.

"What's going on around here, Crafter?" Gameknight asked. "I saw all those soldiers on the village walls, and extra Watchers in the tower. That seemed kinda strange, but then I get down here and see all of your people banging out swords and armor. Hunter's ready to go to war right now. What's going on?"

Crafter looked at Hunter and Stitcher, then pointed up to the circular room at the top of the stairs.

"We should talk up there," he said in a cautious voice, and started up the steps.

The sisters nodded and headed up the stairs, Gameknight following close behind, confused. They reached the top of the steps and moved into the cobblestone-lined room, closing the iron doors behind them.

"What's with all the secrecy?" Gameknight asked.

"Something's going on with the zombies," Crafter said.

"What do you mean something's going on with the zombies? You mean they're sick or something?"

"Sick?" Hunter said, an annoyed look on her face. "You're such an idiot."

"Hunter . . . be nice," Stitcher snapped, slapping her sister on the arm.

"No, not sick," Crafter explained. "We think they're

up to something. The crafters on all the other servers are talking about zombie attacks . . . lots of them. But more importantly, they are infecting the villagers whenever possible."

"Why would they do that?" Gameknight asked as he moved to the center of the room, away from the noise leaking through the iron doors. The others followed.

"We aren't sure. All we know is that they're becoming more violent. And what is even more distressing, they are behaving as if someone is organizing them. It's as if there is a leader amongst them."

"Why is that so surprising?" Gameknight asked. "Why couldn't there be a zombie leader?"

"Zombie-towns have never gotten along with other zombie-towns," Hunter explained as she paced across the room. Without realizing it, she pulled out her enchanted bow, the shimmering weapon adding splashes of sapphire to the grey stone walls. "They always fight amongst themselves like animals, never cooperating or acting like a community."

"Until now," Crafter added. "Someone is getting them to work together, and they are becoming more and more violent. This kind of behavior hasn't happened since the Great Zombie Invasion a hundred years ago."

"Great Zombie Invasion?" Gameknight asked, remembering something about it . . . a book, he'd seen a book in the stronghold library just before their army had journeyed to the End.

"Yes, there was a great invasion of zombies long ago that had cost many lives," Crafter said. "My great great grandfather, Smithy, had led the forces that stopped the invasion. But that had been long ago in a different time. It's disturbing that we're seeing the zombies behave in the same way."

"They're just like a bunch of wild animals and should be put somewhere so that they can't cause any trouble for decent people like us," Hunter said, her voice with a venomous edge. "We don't want them doing to others what they did to my family . . . my village."

She still had not gotten over the destruction of her village and the death of her parents at the hand of Malacoda, the king of the Nether. The terrifying ghast had led an army of monsters from the Nether on a campaign that had ravaged the server she lived on and destroyed many lives, including her parents'. She and her sister Stitcher were all that was left of their village, everyone else dead or Lost.

"Hunter, we must be careful. Before we jump to conclusions, we need to have more information," Stitcher admonished.

Hunter growled, spun around and stormed to the opposite end of the chamber, facing the wall. Her whole body was tense, muscles knotted up like a compressed springs ready to burst.

"What are you going to do?" Gameknight asked.

"The Council of Crafters is going to meet tonight and discuss . . . ahh . . . issues in Minecraft."

"Council of Crafters? What's that?" he asked.

"Crafters can communicate with each other when we are at the limits of Minecraft, down at the level of bedrock or up at the block limit, 256 blocks high," Crafter explained. "At these places, we can reach out and hear each other's thoughts. Tonight, all of the crafters across Minecraft will discuss the situation and decide what to do."

"But maybe this is nothing," Gameknight suggested. "It could just be an insignificant series of random events, you know, like a ripple from a pebble dropped in a pond. The ripples go out in all directions and add to the random motion of the water. Maybe it's nothing."

"My Great Great Uncle Carver once told me of a gigantic wave that crashed down on his sea-side village when he was a young boy," Crafter explained as he stepped closer to his friend. Hunter turned and listened, her bow still clenched in her square fist.

"How could a great wave ever be created in Minecraft?" Gameknight asked. "Waves are caused by the moon . . . by gravity."

"Great Uncle Carver told me that even the smallest of ripples can become great waves if the wind keeps driving them. The smallest, most insignificant of things can become great if a force keeps pushing on it, and that's what happened with his wave."

"What does that have to do with anything?" Hunter asked, her voice sounding agitated, a scowl on her face.

"Perhaps this behavior we're seeing with the zombies is the smallest of ripples, but their new leader could be the wind," Crafter explained. "Over time, this zombie ripple could grow."

"We wouldn't want them to become a great wave," Stitcher added.

"Exactly," Crafter replied.

"THOMAS . . . DINNER," his mother yelled from the basement door.

Gameknight leaned back from the computer and pulled off his gaming headset, then glanced up at the basement steps and sighed.

"OK, MOM, I'M COMING," he yelled, then put his headset back on and moved back to the computer. Pulling the microphone back up to his mouth he spoke to his friends. "I have to go to dinner, but I'll be back as fast as I can."

"When you return, we'll know what the crafters have decided," Crafter said. "I fear things in Minecraft are definitely going to change."

CHAPTER 4
THE WIND

Herobrine moved quietly up behind the user, his eyes glowing bright. As he approached, the hem of his dark smock brushed lightly against the blades of grass, singeing them with the hateful and vile presence that was contained within. The user was bent over a crafting bench, making some kind of wooden tool out here in the open . . . oblivious to his surrounding; what a fool. Moving up right behind him, the shadow-crafter leaned forward and just listened. He could hear the sounds of the Internet leaking through the server thread that stretched up from the user's head and soared upward into the sky, connecting this user to the outside world. Music seeped out of the silvery line, then images and web pages by the thousands, all of them playing like a slide show in the shadow-crafter's mind.

Quietly, he moaned. The feeling of all that freedom just out of reach made him ache and filled him with an unquenchable rage. Herobrine had the faintest of memories still in his mind when he was out there on the Internet, moving from system to system with impunity, but now he was trapped within these foolish Minecraft servers, and he had to get out. The plan for his escape had been botched by the fool of an enderman, Erebus;

all he'd had to do was destroy the Source. But that egotistical enderman has messed up everything by underestimating Gameknight999; Herobrine would not make the same mistake. The path to his salvation, his escape from this confinement, was through the User-that-is-not-a-user and the Gateway of Light, but he had to get him in the right position, and at the right time, in order for his plan to work.

Moving a little nearer, Herobrine listened to the sounds of the Internet in his mind, the volume growing louder and he moved closer to the user. It was delicious . . . all of the possibilities, all of the computers and systems he could infect across the world, if only he could escape this prison. Then he would exact his revenge on those in the physical world.

He laughed.

Suddenly, the user turned around and was shocked to see the bright-eyed Herobrine right behind him. Before the user could react, the dark creature disappeared at the speed of thought and materialized at the bottom of a deep crevasse. He thought about going back and killing that user, but he didn't want to draw attention to himself . . . not yet. Besides, he didn't have a decent sword or any armor.

Just then, he heard the screechy laughter of an enderman. Turning, he could see the dark creature lurking in the shadows, its black skin merging with stone walls.

That's exactly what I need, he thought.

Teleporting to the enderman, he materialized behind the lanky beast. Before the creature could gather its own purple teleportation particles around it, the shadow-crafter started to hit the monster, hammering it with his dark fist. The enderman, confused, turned to confront its attacker, but then Herobrine disappeared and reappeared behind it again. Hitting it in the back, then the side, then the head, he slowly reduced the creature's HP. It tried to fight back, swinging its long skinny arms out, but Herobrine was too fast, and avoided the counterattacks easily. Disappearing and reappearing, he moved about the beast, attacking with a ferocity that the enderman had never seen before. When its HP was nearly zero, the doomed monster collapsed to the ground, its life hanging by a thread.

And that's when Herobrine started to craft. Kneeling next to the monster, he gathered his crafting powers and started to sculpt the creature into something else, converting its computer code into another form. A purplish glow enveloped the enderman as it tried to flee, but the shadow-crafter stopped its teleportation, and focused the purple particles into his crafting, drawing on their energy and turning it to his need. The body of the enderman slowly shrank and drew thinner, the lanky creature slowly changing to a long pointed thing.

Disappearing for just an instant, the shadow-crafter returned with the branch of a tree. While in his grasp, the leaves all shriveled and decayed right before his eyes, each green leaf turning to ash. Shaking the branch to dislodge the dead foliage, he placed the branch on the ground near what was left of the enderman's torso, then continued to craft. Slowly, the shrunken dark body merged with the tree branch until it wasn't possible to tell where the piece of wood ended and the enderman flesh began. With his hands a dark blur, he reformed the creature into the tool that he needed, its body becoming smaller, narrower and pointed, forcing the computer code that defined the enderman into something new. And with a flurry of crafting power, the shadow-crafter finished.

Rising, Herobrine stepped from the shadows of

the wall and moved into the sunlight. In his right hand, he held a pointed sword that was as black as midnight, with a mist of purple particles dancing about its keen edge. Grasping the wooden handle firmly, he swung the blade. It made a whistling sound as the razor-sharp edge cut through the air, a glowing purple trail of light following its path.

A moaning sound echoed through the crevasse. Turning, he saw a zombie approaching, its decaying body staying to the shadows so that it would not burst into flame. Moving quickly to the monster, he swung the blade with all his might. With one blow, the endersword cleaved the life from the creature, destroying it in an instant, leaving behind three spheres of XP. Stepping back, Herobrine made sure he kept far from the XP spheres; he didn't need them . . . not yet.

"Now this is a sword I can work with," the shadow-crafter said, his eyes glowing bright with malice. "But I still need some armor."

Putting the sword in his inventory, he called out a screechy, cackling call that sounded just like an enderman. Instantly, four endermen appeared before him, their eyes darting around, looking for threats.

"Thank you for coming so quickly my friends," the shadow-crafter said in a calm, reassuring voice. "I have need of you, and I appreciate you helping me out."

And then he drew the endersword and slashed at the dark monsters, again bringing them to the brink of destruction. As they fell, gasping for breath, he started to craft again, converting their segments of computer code into something he desperately needed.

"Thank you again for giving me your life force," Herobrine said. "You will make excellent armor . . . enderarmor. And after that is complete, it will be time to set my trap for the User-that-is-not-a-user."

CHAPTER 5
FAMILY

Washing up for dinner, Tommy put on a clean shirt, the one he had been wearing had chocolate milk stains on it (he liked drinking it when he was playing Minecraft). Taking off the shirt, he threw it into the dirty clothes hamper, then chose a new one from his closet. Of course he chose a Minecraft shirt. He thought about getting a custom shirt made that said Gameknight999 on it, but in the physical world he wasn't the User-that-is-not-a-user; in the physical world he was just Tommy Feynman, an unremarkable twelve-year-old kid that wanted to just go through life without being noticed. At school, he'd always had a bully target on his back, until recently. After his adventures in Minecraft, Tommy stood a little taller and was more confident. When the bullies confronted him now, he just changed the situation and reformed the battlefield to his advantage, which usually meant that he just walked away. He also started to notice the patterns; the bullies hung out by the big trashcans in the cafeteria; they were always last to the buses; they were always last to get to class. Knowing the patterns allowed him to plan around them and reduce the possibility of an encounter. This was something he'd learned from his adventures in Minecraft . . . don't be a victim, analyze the situation, change the setting and turn it to your advantage. Because of this, life was now better.

But this was not so for his sister.

Jenny was always getting into some kind of situation at school. She loved art, so much that she didn't really notice people. The other kids called her Art-Geek, and she didn't care. Tommy admired her for her courage and self-confidence, but he also wished she kept it in check sometimes, because it was his responsibility to get her out of the messes she was always getting in; that was his job, to take care of her. Their dad was always saying that 'family takes care of family, no matter what.' And that meant that Tommy had to take care of Jenny at school, even if that meant turning the wrath of the bullies from her and onto him.

Pulling on his creeper t-shirt, Tommy closed his closet. But as the door closed, he could see the box of papers hidden in the back. They were his notes from his adventure in Minecraft. He'd taken to writing down everything that had happened, from the Overworld, to the Nether, and finally to the End and the Source. Tommy wanted to write it all down so that he wouldn't forget what had happened . . . maybe even put it in a book and publish it.

No . . . that's ridiculous, he thought. *That could never happen.*

But the one thing that he'd learned from his adventures in Minecraft with his NPC friend, Crafter, is that the first step toward victory is to accept the idea that success is possible. Once you believe that you can achieve what you want, then all you have to do is keep trying until you succeed. And so he'd keep working on these books until he *was* successful.

"DINNER . . . come on kids," his mom yelled from downstairs.

Pushing his writings to the back of his closet and covering them with his coat, he closed the door and bolted downstairs. He could smell something wonderful on the table, but the real excitement that was building in him was whether his dad would be there or not.

Tommy's dad had been gone on another of his long business trips, trying to sell his inventions. Frequently he'd get home just in time for dinner, if he even came back at all.

"I hope he's here," Tommy muttered to himself.

Sliding down the banister, he landed on both feet and ran for the dining room. As he entered, his heart sank as he saw his father's seat empty, the fourth plate conspicuously absent from the table.

"Come on and sit down," his mom said.

Tommy sat across from Jenny and glared at her. He was still mad because of school today.

"How was school today?" their mother asked as she brought out a platter with meat loaf and veggies on it.

Perfect, Tommy thought. *Let's she what she says.*

"It was fine," Jenny answered.

"FINE?!" Tommy snapped. "She got us in trouble again, Mom."

"Oh I'm sure it wasn't all that bad," Mom replied.

Jenny just smiled.

"It was, Mom," Tommy complained. "She almost got me beat up . . . again."

"What's this?" she asked as she placed the platter on the table.

Jenny grabbed the spoon and took a huge helping of carrots, then took the end slice of the meatloaf. They always competed for the end piece; it was always the crispiest. Poking the piece of meat with her fork, she could hear it crunch . . . it was perfect. Smiling, she stuck her tongue out at Tommy.

"She told Snipes and his cohort, Brandon, to leave another kid alone, and they got really mad."

"I've heard of Brandon . . . I don't like that boy, but who is Snipes?" Mom asked.

"He's the newest of the bullies," Tommy answered. "He's a new kid that just started at our school. His dad was transferred here for work, or something like that. Anyway, he was picking on Jimmy Maxwell and Jenny butted in."

"I couldn't let that kid pick on Jimmy," she said with a mouthful of carrots. "Snipes is twice his size and had all his buddies with him. Funny how the bullies always need their friends with them when they pick on a single individual."

"Mom, she can't keep doing this. Every time she opens her mouth she gets in some kind of trouble, and I have to bail her out," Tommy said. This time, I had to get in front of Snipes and talk him out of beating both of us up."

"I'm sure he wasn't going to hurt you," Mom said as she cut a slice of the meatloaf and put it on Tommy's plate.

Looking down at his plate, he could see that she'd cut into the hard boiled egg that was always at the center of their mom's meatloaf. He'd gotten a huge chunk of the egg. Smiling, he stuck his tongue out at his sister as he speared the egg with his fork and put it into his mouth.

"Of course he would have, Mom!" Tommy objected with his mouth full of egg. "Are you kidding?"

"Don't talk with your mouth full, honey."

Tommy finished chewing and swallowed, then continued.

"He was going to beat me to a pulp, and then start

working on Jenny. I told him that he didn't need to do that. Everyone knew that he was tough and picking on a couple of smaller kids was no challenge from someone as strong as him." He paused to have a gulp of chocolate milk his mom had just poured for him. "He looked me up and down, then I guess figured that we'd be no challenge and walked away."

"You see . . . nothing happened," Jenny added, a huge smile on her face.

"It sounds like everything worked out OK," Mom said.

"But before he walked away he leaned down and whispered to me. He said, 'If your sister gets in the way again, it'll be trouble for both of you.' And then he made a fist and slammed it into his other hand. It sounded like a hammer hitting a piece of steel. Mom, he meant it."

Reaching out, Tommy grabbed the spoon and took another helping of carrots.

"If Jenny keeps sticking her nose in other people's business, eventually she'd going to get hurt. Why can't she just keep quiet?"

"I know that sometimes Jenny can't help herself and she speaks her mind, no matter the consequences," Mom said, "but that is a good thing. If you see something wrong, you should speak up and say something. Remaining silent lets the bullies continue doing what they're doing."

"But why does it always need to be my job to get her out of trouble?"

"Because family always takes care of family . . . no matter what," Mom replied. "And besides, when your father is away, you are . . . "

"Yeah, I know, I'm the man of the house and I have to watch out for my little sister," Tommy said as if reciting a litany from memory. "I've heard Dad say that to me a hundred times, but I'm tired of taking his place here. Why can't he just be at home for a change?"

"You know why, Tommy. Your father is out selling his inventions to support us. He works hard making all of his contraptions, but they don't do us much good if he can't sell them. So when he's away, everybody needs to help out, and that means both of you too."

"I'll try Mom," Jenny replied. "Tommy, tell me more about your friends in Minecraft . . . I wanna hear . . . I wanna hear."

Sighing, Tommy started to describe Crafter, his best friend in Minecraft. Her questions had been becoming more insistent over the last week or so; she was really taking an interest in the game and the characters he'd met. Every chance she had, Jenny interrogated him about the series of events that had occurred, starting with his getting pulled into the game by his father's digitizer and ending with his defending the Source and riding the beam back to the physical world. He didn't mind telling her about his digital friends, in fact he liked talking about them. The NPCs in Minecraft were probably his best friends in the whole world, even though he knew that sounded weird. His mom was confused at first, not sure what to make of Tommy's stories, but he winked so Mom thought he was just making all this up for the benefit of his little sister, Jennifer, even though it had all been true.

"Tell me about the monsters again," Jenny begged.

"Well, there was Erebus, the king of the endermen, and Malacoda, the king of the Nether," Tommy explained. "Erebus was an enderman, tall and scary, and Malacoda was a big ghast. They were both pretty terrifying."

"What about Herobrine?" Jenny asked. "Did you see Herobrine when you were in the game?"

He gave her an exasperated sigh. "Jenny, there is no such thing as Herobrine."

"But I heard that he is . . . "

"I know all the stories . . . that he's the ghost of Notch's dead brother . . . that he sneaks up behind users for some reason . . . that he changes things that other people build . . . that he hates trees . . . I've heard them all."

He grabbed a slice of bread and spread some butter on it, then folded it in half and stuffed the entire piece into his mouth.

"You know," his mother said, "you could take normal sized bites instead of stuffing everything into your mouth at once."

Tommy was going to respond . . . but he had too much bread in his mouth. He gave her a toothy, bread-filled smile, then after chewing and swallowing, he continued. "I've even heard the latest theory, that he's a virus that has infected the game. But every picture I've seen looks like the image was modified, or that Herobrine is so small in the background that you can barely see him. There are no good images of him, no videos . . . nothing."

"But if he isn't real," Jenny argued, "then why do the Minecraft developers deny it so strongly? It's almost as if they are trying to hide something important . . . like it's a conspiracy."

"Jenny, this is just a topic they use to create buzz for the game . . . to keep people playing . . . controversy is always good for sales."

"Well, I think he is real."

"Then you better watch out for him . . . oooooo!" Tommy made a scary face and spooky sounds, then shoved two carrots into his mouth so that they stuck out like orange fangs.

She smiled as she finished her own vegetables.

Turning to his mom, he gave her a wink, suggesting that it was all just a story, then glanced at the vacant chair at the end of the table . . . his father's chair. It was empty. He would've liked to have shown his father all the incredible things he'd learned in the game . . . but he couldn't . . . not today, anyway. Maybe tomorrow . . . that was his mantra.

I wish he were home, I miss my dad, Tommy thought.

Sighing, he gobbled another slice of meatloaf, getting another chunk of the hard boiled egg, then scooped the last bit of carrots into his mouth. Wiping his mouth on his sleeve, he stood up and placed his unused napkin on his plate and carried his dishes to the kitchen sink, then headed for the basement door.

"Mom, I want to play Minecraft with Tommy, but he never lets me," Jenny whined.

"Thomas, you make sure your sister gets to play," his mother said, her voice echoing through the house as only a mom's voice could.

"But it's her turn to do the dishes," Tommy protested, then smiled. That would give him time to get back in and talk with his friends before she finished.

"That is true," Mom said. "I see it on the chores list, it is her turn."

"But Mommmm," she whined.

Tommy smiled. He knew he had her trapped and there was no escape from the jaws of the chores list.

"I'll be in the basement," he shouted as he streaked down the wooden stairs.

CHAPTER 6

THE NEW ORDER

In seconds, he was logged back into Minecraft. Gameknight999 spawned back at his original hidey-hole. He didn't expect that. It was as if something had been reset in the game . . . strange. Checking his inventory, he headed for Crafter's village, anxious to hear about the Council of Crafters. As he streaked across the landscape, he saw numerous spiders and creepers, but also saw more zombies than expected, the rotting creatures hiding in the shade of trees or in the dark recesses of caves that opened to the surface.

This worried him.

Why would there be so many zombies out in the daytime? Normally, they stay hidden away during the day, hiding wherever zombies hide, for they would burst into flames if sunlight were to touch their skin. But it seemed that the zombies were getting braver, and that was disconcerting.

Ignoring the monsters, Gameknight stayed his course and headed for Crafter's village. As he ran, he could start to see the fortified outer wall show itself over the gentle rolling hills. The barricade of cobblestone looked strong from this distance, with alternating blocks lining the top like boxy teeth; protection for the archers that guarded their perimeter. He could remember when they had built that wall, before the first real battle with Erebus, the king of the endermen. The walls and the traps that they'd constructed within the village had turned back the tide of monsters that

were crashing down on the village and delivered the
first defeat to the monsters of the Overworld. That
was when the war to save Minecraft really began.

He could remember how proud the villagers
had been at the defense of their village. The NPCs had
stood strong, weapons in hand, and faced down
their ancient enemies, staring down their fears and
refusing to yield. And this had had a lasting impact on
the villagers. He could still remember the day when
he'd released their hands so that they could take up
the defense of their land. Normally, NPCs have their
hands linked across their chests, their hands tucked
up into their sleeves; but Gameknight999, the User-
that-is-not-a-user, had accidently discovered a way
to release their hands and let them take up weapons.
It had changed their lives, and when word got out,
all the NPCs across all the Minecraft servers had
their hands free to use. To this day, they stood taller,
stronger, unafraid of challenges because they knew
that success *was* possible, that they could face a
terrifying enemy and stand together to defeat it. But
as he neared the village, Gameknight noticed that
things looked different. He could see the warriors
walking the parapet, guarding the perimeter, but
they didn't look as strong and threatening as he
remembered. And then he realized what it was—they
had no weapons. And their hands . . . he couldn't
see their hands. Their arms were locked across their
chests again, hands hidden within sleeves.

What is going on? he thought.

As he neared, the iron gates swung open, a villager
standing on the nearby pressure plate allowed him
access. Stepping into the large gravel entrance, he saw
villagers walking about, doing their jobs, but none of
them were using their hands; they were all hidden
within sleeves. And instead of shouting out his name,

they all just stopped and stared at him, some of them bowing slightly. He could see many of them glance up at the server thread that stretched up from his head. The thin white stream of light shot upward from his body, soaring high up into the sky, connecting Gameknight999 to the server . . . and the Source. He wasn't the User-that-is-not-a-user anymore, he realized. No, the server thread made him just another user out for a stroll through Minecraft. But even with that being true, these NPCs all knew him from sight, and knew him well . . . yet they looked at him like he was a stranger.

Something's happened . . . but what?

Gameknight approached one of the NPCs. By the look of his clothes, he was a baker, his smock brown with a wide stripe of white running down the center.

"What's happening? Is there something wrong?" Gameknight asked.

Baker just looked back at him, a sad look on his boxy face, but said nothing. Turning, he saw a child running up to him, their hands also concealed, arms linked across their chest. It was one of Digger's kids; he recognized him right away . . . Topper.

But now he could see that something was definitely wrong. Instead of Topper wrapping his short little arms around his waist, he was just standing next to him, leaning his head against his stomach. Looking down, Gameknight put his hand on the boy's shoulder, causing the young NPC to look up at him.

"What's wrong, Topper?" Gameknight asked. "Why won't anyone talk to me?"

The boy said nothing, just looked up at his hero, the User-that-is-not-a-user. Kneeling down, he looked at Topper straight in the eyes.

"What's wrong?"

Topper just stared back, a sad, sad look on his

face. Then a blocky tear started to form at the corner of one of his small square brown eyes. It trickled down his cheek, leaving behind a rectangular streak of wetness across his blocky cheek. A grunting sound came from across the square. He could see Digger's blocky forming coming toward them, his brown and grey smock swinging as he walked. He grunted something in their ancient testificate language, then gestured with his head to their home. Topper looked up at Gameknight, then scurried toward their home.

Digger looked at Gameknight, then turned and headed toward the center of the village. Stopping for a moment, he turned to make sure that Gameknight was following. Grunting again, he motioned with his head for him to follow, then sprinted toward the center of the village. Gameknight sighed as he watched Topper disappear into their home, then followed Digger toward the center of town, toward the tall rocky tower-like structure that loomed high above the village.

I must find out what is going on, Gameknight thought. *And for that, I need to talk to Crafter . . . but will he talk to me?*

Gameknight shuddered as they entered the cobblestone tower that stood watch over the village. Moving to the far corner of the ground floor, Digger stood next to the secret entrance that led down into their underground crafting chambers and minecart network. Pulling out his diamond pickaxe, Gameknight swung it down hard, shattering the cobblestone block with three quick blows, and exposing the long tunnel. Looking up at Digger, he sighed, then stepped onto the ladder and slid down into the darkness.

CHAPTER 7

WHISPERS IN THE DARK

Gameknight reached the bottom of the tunnel then looked back up. He could see Digger looking down at him, backlit by the torches that lined the ground floor of the watchtower. And then the top of the tunnel went dark as Digger placed a block of cobblestone into the floor, sealing it.

Turning, he headed for the circular chamber, hoping that he would find his friend Crafter there. Sprinting as fast as he could, he reached the chamber in a minute, his mind full of questions. But as he entered the room, he found it empty . . . no Crafter. Sighing, he moved to the two iron doors that guarded the crafting chamber. Banging on the door with his diamond pick, he peeked through the window. Instantly, he saw all activity cease, as those that were crafting something for Minecraft all stopped, their hands tucked into their sleeves. One of the iron clad warriors whose job it was to guard the door approached and looked at Gameknight through the embedded window, then shook his head, a sad look on his face.

They aren't going to let me in, he thought. *This is ridiculous!*

Moving next to the door, he swung his diamond pickaxe and smashed through the cobblestone that supported the door. The blocks fell easily under his attack, causing the door to also fall to the ground. The guard just stood there as Gameknight entered the crafting chamber. He knew that all of the guards now carried swords; they had become very skilled in their use, but no one raised a hand to stop him.

Glancing down at the floor of the chamber, he could see Crafter standing with some of the other NPCs, his small form clothed in a black smock that stood out against the other grey-clad NPCs. He had a look of importance about him that did not match his size. It was something about the look on his face, his bright blue eyes filled with years and years of experience and wisdom, though his body held the smallest portion of those years.

Crafter had, at one time, been an old, grey-haired NPC; he'd probably been the oldest NPC on all the Minecraft servers. But during that terrible battle to save this server and stop the monsters of the Overworld, Crafter had been killed. Fortunately, he had absorbed enough XP to respawn on the next server, reappearing in his current childish form. All NPCs could tell by the look in his eyes that he was not a child, but likely the wisest NPC in Minecraft, and Gameknight had learned not to underestimate that wisdom. That was important because right now, he needed answers about what was going on.

Moving down the steps that led to the floor, Gameknight ran past NPCs, their eyes following his progress. They all knew where he was heading. Leaping down the last few steps, and taking a small amount of damage from the fall, Gameknight bolted straight toward his friend.

"Crafter, what's going on? What with all the villager's hands? Why won't anyone talk to me?"

Gameknight looked deep into his friend's eyes and waited for an answer . . . he received none, just a sad look and a shaking head.

"What's happening?!"

Crafter looked about the chamber at all the

NPCs watching this encounter, then looked back at Gameknight999 and shook his head.

Gameknight glanced about the room and saw all the eyes watching them, then came up with an idea. Pulling out his pickaxe, he moved to the wall of the crafting chamber, then started to dig. He bored straight into the flesh of Minecraft, digging a two-by-two tunnel that pierced the wall and went in about ten blocks deep. Collecting the stone, which now turned to cobblestone in his inventory, he moved back to Crafter. Pulling out his shovel, he used it to gently push Crafter toward the tunnel.

"Go . . . into the tunnel," Gameknight commanded.

Crafter looked about at the other NPCs, a helpless look on his face.

"Don't look at them, they can't help you . . . now go, into the tunnel."

Gameknight kept pushing his friend with the tool. He felt bad about doing this, but he knew that this was the only way to get some answers.

Reluctantly, Crafter allowed himself to be pushed into the tunnel. Once in the passageway and out of sight from the others, he turned and walked all the way to the end of the rocky passage. Once he reached the tunnel's end, he turned and faced Gameknight999.

Pulling out blocks of cobblestone, Gameknight started to seal in the passage, filling in three layers of cobblestone in the tunnel to keep them isolated from those in the crafting chamber. Instantly, they were plunged into darkness. He then pulled out a few torches and placed them on the walls, spilling light throughout the makeshift room.

"Now . . . talk," Gameknight said in a whisper.

Crafter looked about the room, then moved to the far end of the tunnel, as far from the crafting chamber as possible. Gameknight stepped up next to his friend and looked down at him.

"The Council of Crafter . . . they made a decision," Crafter said in a quiet, airy voice, his whisper barely audible.

"A decision about what?" Gameknight asked, his voice becoming louder as his frustration built.

Crafter looked up at him with scared eyes, then looked about the small room.

"Sorry," Gameknight whispered. "What was the decision about?"

"There has been trouble with zombies," Crafter continued. "They have been attacking villages all across the server planes, infecting more and more NPCs. It's as if they want to increase their numbers for some reason."

"You think it's another zombie invasion, like the one you mentioned that happened long ago?"

"That's what many of the crafters believe. It is everyone's hope that this is not the case, that everything can go back to normal."

"But what's normal?" Gameknight asked. "Everything changed since the Last Battle. Why would zombies be attacking all the villages like this, unprovoked? It doesn't makes sense."

"Many feel the problem is that Minecraft was changed . . . by you."

"By me?"

Crafter nodded.

"But I tried to save Minecraft!"

"I know, you changed Minecraft so that we could save ourselves. Everyone knows this and everyone is grateful, but many believe that things should go back to the way they were before Erebus and Malacoda."

"Go back . . . I don't understand."

Crafter pulled his hands out of his sleeves and held them up into the air as if showing them to his friend.

He then put them back, linking his arms against his chest.

"It has been decided by the Council that NPCs cannot talk with users, and cannot be seen using their hands by users . . . like it was before . . . "

"Before the User-that-is-not-a-user."

Crafter nodded, then continued. "It was decided that anyone with a server thread must be kept from the secrets of Minecraft."

"You mean that nobody can know that you are alive."

Crafter nodded.

"And nobody can find out that you know how to use your hands."

He nodded again, this time a look of sadness spreading across his square face.

"And you can't talk to anyone that has a . . . "

Gameknight stopped speaking as realization of what he was saying slowly percolated through his mind, he then looked down at his friend and a pain greater than anything he'd experienced in Minecraft spread through him: the pain of lost friendships . . . and absent friends.

"You mean that we can't . . . "

Crafter nodded as he used his sleeve to wipe away a tear from his square cheek.

"But . . . we're . . . I mean they can't just . . . "

"It was decided, it's done," Crafter said, his voice choked with emotion. "If anyone is seen breaking the laws, then they will be kicked out of their village and forced to be one of the Lost, a village-less NPC."

"They'll be forced to wonder through Minecraft until they find a village to take them . . . but none will, right?"

Crafter didn't respond, but Gameknight knew the answer to his question.

"So the punishment for violating this rule is essentially death, is that right?" Gameknight asked.

Crafter nodded again, then looked down at the ground, ashamed. "It's done. When we leave this tunnel, we will not be able to communicate ever again."

The words slammed into Gameknight999 like a broadsword. His friends . . . gone . . . it wasn't right. He wanted to complain to someone, to yell and scream, but it wouldn't matter. Their decision would not change. This was the end of Minecraft as Gameknight knew it, and it felt like someone had stabbed him in the heart.

"We started as strangers in this village," Crafter said as he looked up at Gameknight999, "and then we ended as best friends. It is sad that all things that begin must end. I will sorely miss our times together."

Gameknight looked at his friend and was filled with anger. How could this be . . . it wasn't right. He tried to feel for the pieces of the puzzle, looking for a solution to this problem, but there was nothing there, no clever idea, no trick to get around this . . . just sadness, overwhelming sadness.

"It is time to go," Crafter said softly, pointing to the cobblestone wall.

Drawing out his pick, Gameknight swung it at the blocks. All of his rage was focused into that wall, every bit of anger over the injustice of the situation, over the foolishness of this decision . . . all of his emotions were focused into the stone blocks. In seconds, the diamond pickaxe tore through the wall as if it were made of paper, leaving small cubes floating on the ground that zipped into his inventory. When the last block was removed, Gameknight turned and looked back at his friend for the last time, then turned to leave. But suddenly, he bumped into another user.

"Hi Tommy," said the voice of a young girl.

Gameknight glanced above the girl's head and saw the name Monet113 floating in the air, the letters glowing a bright white.

It was his sister.

"What are you doing here?" he snapped.

"Mom said I could use the laptop to play Minecraft," she explained. "So I logged in and teleported to you. Is that Crafter behind you? . . . he looks just like how you described him."

Gameknight looked over his shoulder at Crafter then back at his sister.

"Yeah . . . that's . . . "

She shoved past her brother and stood right in front of Crafter.

"Hi Crafter, my name is Jenny, I'm Tommy's sister and . . . "

"Don't use real names online . . . "

"Oh yeah . . . sorry. My name is Monet113 and I'm Gameknight999's sister. It's a pleasure to meet you Crafter."

The young boy in the black smock said nothing, just looked straight ahead.

She looked at Crafter for a minute, then turned back to her brother.

"What's wrong?" Monet113 asked. "Why won't he talk with me?"

"He isn't allowed to talk with users anymore."

"What do you mean?!" Monet asked, her voice piercing in Gameknight's headset.

"They've decided that things . . . " he sniffled, "have to go back to the way they were before the war. That means no talking with users."

"But that's not fair, I mean they could . . . "

"Just leave it alone!" Gameknight snapped.

She could tell by the tone of his voice that he wasn't playing around. Stepping back, she moved out of the tunnel and out of the way. Gameknight walked out of the passage, feeling all the eyes in the crafting chamber on him. He could see the sad, sympathetic looks on all of the NPC's faces but knew that there was nothing anyone could do. This was just Minecraft . . . now . . . just another silly computer game.

He stopped for a moment and looked over his shoulder at his friend. Crafter's big blue eyes were looking back at him, filled with sadness. But then it looked as if the young NPC were about to say something . . .

Suddenly, an NPC, one of the watchers, burst into the crafting chamber. She ran down the stairs and stopped right in front of Crafter, but turned to look at Gameknight and Monet. Clearly she wanted to say something but was forbidden, so she just stood there looking agitated.

"Come on sis', let's go," Gameknight said as he headed out of the crafting chamber, his little sister in tow.

They reached the surface in silence, but when they exited the watchtower they found the village in chaos. The villagers were running about in a panic, their hands tucked into their sleeves, arms linked across their chests.

"What's going on?" Gameknight asked one villager.

The NPC just shook his head.

He turned to another and interrogated them, and received the same answer. Turning to look across the gravel square he saw Digger. Running to him, Gameknight stopped directly in front of the NPC and stared directly into his eyes.

"Digger, what's happening?"

Digger looked around and could see that there were many eyes on him. He then looked up at the walls and ran, leading Gameknight to the stairs that led to the top of the barricade. Following the NPC,

Gameknight was still confused. The villagers were acting as if they were terrified, but what was there to be terrified of?

And then he reached the top of the barricade and understood their fear. Out on the rolling hills that surrounded the village was a large cluster of spiders, a few creepers in their midst.

Drawing his enchanted bow, he fired a few arrows to get the range, then aimed for the creepers. If he could get them to ignite, then maybe they would take some of the spiders with them. But he noticed that his arrows were the only ones flying.

"Why aren't you firing?" he yelled to the other archers atop the wall. "Shoot for the creepers."

But the villagers all stood there, staring at him. Some glanced nervously at the approaching spiders, but none of them drew their weapons, their hands still uselessly linked within their sleeves.

"You have to fight . . . NOW!"

No response, only sad, scared eyes looking back at him.

And then Crafter was at his side. He gently bumped into him, making Gameknight turn around. Spinning, he found Crafter had a sign in his hands. It said something but he couldn't quite see until he placed it on a block. The sign had just three words, but they delivered a powerful message that crushed him as if he were in a vise.

"You must go!"

Gameknight looked down at the sign, then back up at Crafter. He understood the message; they couldn't defend themselves if a user was here. The NPCs would rather let the monsters into their village, than violate the law that had been decreed by the Council of Crafters.

Gameknight sighed . . . this was truly the end.

Looking over his shoulder, he saw his sister and ran down to her.

"We have to leave," he said.

"What? . . . but there's going to be a battle . . . I want to watch."

"If we stay here, then the villagers cannot defend themselves, and they will die. These are living creatures, not just pieces in a game to be toyed with." He turned to look up at Crafter who still stood up on the wall, then turned back to his sister. "It's time to go . . . you first."

"Ohhhh . . . OK," Monet said reluctantly.

Her character froze for a moment, then disappeared with a flash that seemed to streak upward as her server thread withdrew back up into the sky. Gameknight then turned to Crafter and waved to his friend for probably the last time, then disconnected from Minecraft.

CHAPTER 8

THE CRAFTING OF XA-TUL

He isn't here," Herobrine muttered to himself as he walked out of the zombie village.

He'd just finished explaining to this rabble of zombies what their new task in life was to be . . . to make the NPCs suffer until they gave him what he wanted: the User-that-is-not-a-user. They didn't accept his leadership right away. Unfortunate, but they always refuse . . . at first. It forced him to demonstrate the efficiency of his new endersword on a few of the zombie elders. However, after ten or fifteen examples, the zombie village became quite reasonable.

He chuckled . . . zombies, they are so pathetically weak. Destroy a few of them and they all just fall in line . . . so predictable.

But now he needed to move to a new server to look for his prey. Normally, he would just gather his own shadow-crafting powers and create a doorway that would take him through the Source and to a new server, but it took a lot of energy and it always left him feeling incredibly weak and vulnerable. And he did not like feeling vulnerable, even though there was nothing on any of these servers that could possibly challenge him . . . well, except for the User-that-is-not-a-user, but he hasn't felt his presence on any of the servers since the Last Battle.

He'll be back, Herobrine thought, *this Gameknight999 cannot help himself.*

As he walked out of the dark tunnel and into the sunlight, he saw a user in the distance. He was building some kind of redstone contraption, something with pistons and pressure plates.

These users don't understand the true power within Minecraft, he thought. *They are just as foolish as the NPCs.*

Gathering his shadow-crafting powers, he created a doorway and stepped through, materializing right behind the user. Instantly, he was treated to the sounds of the Internet leaking through the user's server thread. Images of kittens doing cute things, telephone conversations, financial transactions, machine control signals, missile defense codes being tested . . . a myriad of things moving through the Internet all at once. It was delicious . . . all those people, all that potential, all that freedom . . . all of it just outside the confines of these ridiculous servers. He had to get out . . . had to find the User-that-is-not-a-user and escape this prison.

When I move into the Internet, I will take it all over, and then I will make the users suffer, Herobrine thought. *I will disrupt their communication, sabotage their control systems, and interrupt their lives in every way possible. I will rule their world from the creation of their own making, the Internet. They were foolish to connect everything to the Internet. Even their military machines are on this network. Soon, I will finish what I had that poor servant Erebus start. But first I need a new servant . . . a new hero to continue where Erebus and that fool, Malacoda, failed.*

Reaching up, the shadow-crafter grasped the user's server thread. In that instant, the user turned around and was surprised to find a bright-eyed shadow-crafter standing right behind him. Drawing his endersword, Herobrine swung it over the head of the user, severing the server thread and disconnecting him from the server. In that instance, when the anchor to this server was removed, the server thread snapped back up to the Source, pulling the shadow-crafter back with it, allowing him to jump through the Source and to a new server without consuming any of his energy.

When he materialized, he felt excited. He hadn't been certain if that was going to work, but it functioned perfectly. He was able to move from the last server to this one without feeling weak or vulnerable . . . fantastic!

And then he felt it, a distant ripple in the fabric of Minecraft. The shadow-crafter knelt down and pressed his ear to the grassy plan, and listened. He could hear it! There was the faintest of echoes that still lingered within the music of Minecraft. Gameknight999 had been on this server.

Finally, he'd found his trail.

Surveying his surroundings, he found that he had materialized within a Mega Taiga biome, tall pine trees stretching high up into the air, so tall that he could barely see their peaks. Nearby, he could see patches of dirt with no grass growing, small brown mushrooms sprouting in the shadows. Blocks of mossy stone were clustered here and there, standing out against the brown of the forest floor. They reminded him of the wonderful dungeons that his shadow-crafters liked to put here and there to tempt the foolish users. They never think to bring milk with them when they explore these spaces, milk being the only antidote to the cave spider venom.

He laughed, but then grew silent as the wailing howl of a wolf sounded off to his left in the forest. And then another replied off to the right, then another and another. They'd sensed him.

"I hate wolves," he muttered to himself.

They always seem to be on the lookout for him, instantly attacking him whenever they found him. He could easily defend himself against a small or medium-sized pack, especially now that he had his endersword. They were just an annoyance but he'd rather not be distracted right now. There were important things to be done.

Opening another doorway, he stepped through and materialized in the mouth of a cave that extended deep into the bowels of Minecraft. Walking through the cave and connecting tunnels, he searched for the zombie village that he knew was hidden nearby. The sounds of other monsters echoed in the cave, the clicking of spiders and the swish-swish of creeper feet. But they were wise enough to stay far from Herobrine.

Moving deeper into the tunnel network, he started to smell smoke and ash . . . the smell of home. Running through the rocky passageway, he continued to descend until he reached the level of lava . . . wonderful, glorious lava. Walking along the edge of a lava river, he followed the flow for maybe forty blocks until he started to hear the sound he was searching for, the splashing of water . . . a waterfall. In the distance, he could see a stream of water flowing out of a hole in the wall, the blue column falling down into the lava, forming cobblestone and obsidian.

This was the place.

Scanning the walls, he found what he was looking for, a section of wall that was flat, just a single block of stone sticking out. Jumping across the lava river, he reached up to press the lone block, but then stopped as the sound of zombie wails reached his ears. Their sorrowful cries filled the passageway with the sadness of their race . . . forever banned from the sunlight because of their past transgressions and now just relegated to the shadows, the blue sky just a distant memory.

A group of six zombies were approaching.

"Thank you for coming, friends," he said to the zombies.

The monsters looked confused.

"I need your help to craft my new servant, no, my new hero," Herobrine said, a wry smile on his face. "And your sacrifice will go down in history as the thing that let me finally escape my prison . . . you should be proud."

One of the zombies looked at his comrades, then turned to Herobrine.

"What is this shadow-crafter saying?" the zombie grumbled in its guttural, almost animal-sounding voice.

"You will see," Herobrine answered, then disappeared and reappeared right next to the group.

Drawing his endersword, he slashed out at the helpless monsters, tearing their HP from them with painful sweeps of his sword. The monsters instantly fell, each just barely alive.

Putting his sword aside, Herobrine reached out to the wounded zombies and, drawing on all of his crafting powers, began to shift the computer code that governed these creatures, pushing the lines of code into new directions. Instantly, his hands started to glow a sickly yellow, like the color of a dying flower, as he crafted these creatures into something new. Looking down at his work, Herobrine could see the lines of software start to merge, the tangle of machine commands weaving together into a complex tapestry of digital instructions. As he crafted, the bodies of the monsters began to overlap and flow together, gradually morphing into a new creature that was bigger, taller, and stronger than its forefathers. Nearing completion, Herobrine saw some blocks of iron nearby and reached out to add these to his creation. Drawing the iron into thin strands of wire, he wove the metal into small links of chain. Laying the chain mail over the body, he attached it to the creature with his crafting power, his hand now glowing almost bright white. He then infused his own loathsome hatred for the NPCs of the Overworld and that pathetic Gameknight999. Pouring every bit of his vile, evil nature into the creature, he finished his creation.

And as the light from his hands slowly faded, he stood and stepped back to admire his handiwork. The creature lay on the ground, apparently asleep. Giving it a strong kick in the ribs, he brought the creature into consciousness. Standing up, the gigantic zombie loomed over Herobrine, its rotting skin hanging off in flaps, exposing bones peeking out from under its tattered clothes. Cautiously, it took its first step forward, the chain mail that covered its body jingled and clinked as it swayed on its terrifyingly huge fame.

"Come, my child, step forward and let me see you," Herobrine said.

The monster moved forward into the light of the lava river. It was the biggest zombie Herobrine had ever seen in Minecraft, a normal zombie only coming up to this creature's shoulders. Its arms was thick and muscular, like two dangerous cannons ready to go off, but the most wonderful part of all was its claws. Herobrine could see the razor-sharp claws on each hand, each claw looking more like a lethal dagger, the points shining in the lava light. These claws would be able to cut through iron as if it were butter . . . the User-that-is-not-a-user would not stand a chance.

Herobrine laughed.

"Master," the monster said in its scratchy voice.

"Yes my child," Herobrine answered.

"Master, what is my name?"

Herobrine thought for a moment, then drew a name from ancient zombie history. This would make the crafters of the Overworld quiver in their boots and wish they had never resisted him.

"I shall name you Xa-Tul," Herobrine said, then gave his creation an eerie, toothy smile. "Now come, we have much to do and many creatures to destroy."

And then Herobrine laughed a maniacal, evil laugh that made the stone walls around them cringe with terror.

CHAPTER 9
MONET113

The next morning, Jenny got up early. She wanted to beat her brother to the basement computer: that one had the best graphics and was the fastest. Besides, playing Minecraft on the laptop just wasn't the same as playing it on their dad's computer. Shooting down the stairs two at a time, she raced to the desk in the corner and sat down.

Her brother must have left Minecraft on last night, because she could see it on the screen . . . but it looked different. He'd been messing with making his own mods recently, and maybe he had been testing one late last night before he went up to bed. She wasn't sure, and she didn't care. Jenny just wanted to get into the game and talk with Crafter and all of Gameknight's friends. She knew that they wouldn't talk to users, her brother had made that perfectly clear, and as upset as he was after logging out, Jenny knew that it must have been true.

But she had a plan.

Logging in with her user ID, Monet113, her character materialized into the game. But instead of looking at what had formed into Minecraft, she instead turned around and rolled her chair over to the controller for her father's invention, the digitizer.

"Tommy had gone into Minecraft with the digitizer and gotten out OK," she said to the empty basement, "so I should be able to do that too."

She'd seen her father use the digitizer lots of

times and knew right where the switches were that would activate the device. Turning on the power, then charging the capacitors, she brought the thing to life. The raygun-looking device started to glow a soft yellow as a buzzing sound began to fill the basement, the end of the digitizer pointing straight at her. And as the buzzing sound grew louder, she turned to face the computer screen, ready to pass through the Gateway of Light. But just before the mechanism blasted her with a white hot beam of light, she saw her Minecraft character on the screen. Looking back at her from the computer monitor was not the character she expected. Instead of being clothed in dark blue, with a splash of purple across her torso and light blue hair spilling down her head and shoulders, she saw the image of a zombie child, its rotting body and tattered clothes looking as if they were about to all fall apart.

"Zombie . . . why does it look like a . . . "

And then the beam of light enveloped her, wrapping its blazing hot fingers around the very fabric of her being. Tingling sensations spread all across her body, making it feel as if her skin were burning, but at the same time terribly cold. Jenny could barely make out the details of the basement through the blaze of white light, but the features started to spin as the buzzing grew louder and the light brighter. It felt as if she were caught in a tornado and she were stuck in the center, the room zooming past her and a hundred miles an hour. At first it felt as if the light were hammering her from the outside, wrapping itself around her skin with its luminous coat. But then the burning, chilling sensation started to radiate from within her as the digitizer started to envelop every part of her life force. She could feel herself being pulled down the digital drain at the bottom of this bathtub they called reality. It felt as if Jenny were being wrenched apart, her mind and memories and emotions being drawn through from the physical world and pulled into the 1s and 0s of the digital realm.

And then things went dark as Monet113 slowly faded into unconsciousness, but just as the darkness wrapped itself around her mind, she thought she could hear animals: chickens, cows, and pigs . . . oh my.

As she opened her eyes, Monet found that she was lying face down in a field of grass. Sitting up, she looked around. Behind her was a large hill, a rocky outcropping sticking out into the air, a waterfall flowing from its peak. A breeze flowed across the landscape, making the blades of grass wave gently, the sweet fragrance of flowers reaching her senses. Everything looked so real, the features of the grass and trees and hills and sky; it was all so beautiful.

Monet113 reached down to pick a white flower that sat at her feet, but as she extended her hand, she saw needle-sharp claws on the end of her blocky fingers.

Claws? she thought, *why would I have claws?*

And then she looked down at her arms. They were a mottled, faded green that reminded her of blocks of cheese left too long in the refrigerator. The sleeves to her shirt were tattered and torn, the light blue material looking as if it had been wrung out a few hundred times too many. Standing, she looked down at her legs. They were clothed in blue pants that were also tattered and stained.

I'm confused . . . what happened?

Looking at the pool of water into which the waterfall flowed, she moved toward it, hoping to see her reflection. As soon as Monet started to walk, her arms instantly came up and stretched out in front of her, sparkling dark claws extended. She tried to pull her arms down, but found it difficult while she was walking, their stiffness somehow linked to her shuffling feet.

Reaching the watery pool, she looked down at her reflection and was shocked at what she saw . . . she was a zombie child! Somehow, Monet113 had spawned as a zombie child rather than in her normal, colorful skin.

"How did this happen?" she said aloud to no one . . . to Minecraft.

And then a clicking sound echoed off the hills. It was a sound she knew all too well from her many hours in Minecraft; it was a spider.

Spinning around, Monet found herself standing face to face with a giant spider, its multiple red eyes glaring at her with suspicious intent.

Is it going to attack me? she thought as waves of fear crashed down upon her.

Glancing down, she could see the curved wicked-looking claws at the end of each leg, their razor-sharp points gleaming in the sunlight. Looking up, Monet could see all the tiny black hair that covered the creature's body moving in every direction at once. It was as if each stubby black strand had a mind of its own . . . it was creepy. Shuddering, she brought her attention back to the terrifying face. It clicked its thick curved mandibles together, the curved horn-like structures that sat on either side of its hideous mouth looked like they could cut through steel. She shuddered again as waves of fear flowed down her spine.

What am I going to do? she thought, then her mind settled on an idea. *What would my brother do? I know . . . he'd fight!*

Reaching into her inventory, she wasn't sure how, Monet113 searched for some kind of weapon or tool or anything that she could defend herself with, but found nothing. The spider scuttled to the side and looked her all over, moving its gigantic head up close. Its blazing red eyes shifted in every direction at once as it inspected her, then they all turned upward to look above her head; the creature was likely looking for her server thread. If this monster found it, then she was in big trouble. The monster then circled around her and came back to her front and stared up into her dark eyes. Satisfied this was just another zombie, the monster left, its mandibles clicking together as it moved through the long grass.

"That was close," she said with a scratchy, grumbly voice.

"What was close?" another voice said from behind.

Turning, Monet found herself facing another zombie child. She was dressed exactly like her, tattered light blue shirt, torn dark blue pants, but her face looked subtly different. Her eyes were dark like Monet's but with a hint of green to them. She could see deep scars on her face and arms, some of them looking like they were freshly scratched into her skin.

"Noticing the scars on this zombie's arms?" the zombie girl asked, a ring of pride in her voice. "Battle training has begun . . . it is hoped that more scars will joins these, soon."

"What?" Monet said.

"Battle training . . . zombie battle training . . . oh, perhaps this new zombie has not started it yet? That's OK, it will begin soon. What level?"

"What . . . I don't understand."

The zombie girl moved closer, her dark claws sparkling in the sunlight. Monet wanted to step back but knew she needed to stand her ground and not look suspicious.

"What's the new zombie's name?" the girl asked. "This zombie is called Ba-Jin."

"My name is Monet11 . . . ah . . . I mean my name is Monet."

"Mo-Nay . . . the new zombie is a Mo? Wow!"

Ba-Jin was impressed, but Monet didn't understand why. She was just about to ask when a moaning sound drifted across the landscape.

"Zombies must get back," Ba-Jin said. "The elders do not like the younglings to be out in the sun too long."

"Ah . . . yeah . . . of course," Monet answered.

Zombies were afraid of the sunlight as adult zombies would burst into flames. Zombie children, however, were immune to the burning effects of the sun and could be out during the day. *But apparently the other zombies don't like them to be out for very long*, Monet thought.

Following her new friend, Monet113 walked toward the shadows of the trees where she could see more zombies milling about, their arms outstretched. They were all dressed identically, light blue shirt, dark blue pants . . . it was as if they all tried to be exactly like each other. However, as she scanned the crowd of zombies, Monet noticed subtle differences: this one with scars across a cheek, that one with a limp, another with skin a little darker than the rest; there were differences here, but it seemed as if the zombies wanted those differences to be hidden behind identical clothing . . . interesting.

One of the adults gave her and Ba-Jin a disapproving scowl, their dark beady eyes boring into her as if something was not right. Monet knew that they couldn't see her server thread; she'd use the digitizer so she didn't have a server thread, but maybe they could see letters over her head? As they followed the adults through the dense forest, they passed by a pool of water. Moving to the pond's edge, she looked down at her watery reflection. Staring back at her from the watery depths was a zombie child; its skin green and decaying but with the faintest wisps of color here and there, making her subtly different from the other child. Her eyes looked cold and dead, colored black like the inside of her closet with the lights out. On her boxy head she saw no hair, but there was a streak of blue across the right side, likely a remnant of her original Minecraft skin. Looking closer, Monet113 could see some letters floating just above her head, but they were made with some kind of transparent font so that light passed through them; they were nearly invisible. If someone looked carefully, they might notice them . . . she had to be careful. It would be important to not draw attention to herself. Who knows what the zombies would do if they realized that she were a user, or worse, a User-that-is-not-a-user.

Shuddering as the potential danger of the situation settled around her mind like a suffocating blanket, she moved away from the water and followed the zombies toward Zombie-town.

CHAPTER 10

THE SEEDS OF
THE STORM

Herobrine and Xa-Tul silently materialized at the mouth of the large cave, just popping into existence on this new server in hopes of finding that annoying Gameknight999. Instantly, Herobrine could feel that Gameknight999 was not here and had never been on this server; the echoing ripples of his passage were completely absent. This was the wrong server.

"I'll find you yet, Gameknight999," he muttered to himself.

"What?" grumbled Xa-Tul in a deep voice that sounded like scratchy thunder.

"Nothing . . . he is not here," Herobrine answered. "Go and instruct your subjects. Be quick about it. I will wait here."

"Yes, master."

Xa-Tul walked into the cave and followed the jagged tunnels down into the darkness. He could feel the presence of other monsters in the shadows, but they all feared him, his size unnatural and terrifying, even to his own kind. Ignoring their presence, he closed his eyes and opened himself up to the music of Minecraft. He could hear all the different creatures scurrying about through the tunnels, the spiders clicking their mandibles apprehensively, the creepers looking for something to explode, and the zombies aimlessly shuffling about without purpose. Well, he'd give them purpose soon enough. Reaching back into his memories, he felt for the location of the zombie-town. Though he'd only been alive for hours, he still carried the memories of those zombies that gladly gave their lives for him to be created. And then he found it . . . the collision of fire and water, that's what he needed . . . that's where the entrance to zombie-town would be found.

Following the tunnel before him, he continued to descend. At times he ran into dead ends, the tunnels abruptly ending; that was how Minecraft sometimes created these tunnels. With his mighty fists, he smashed through stone walls when he could sense a passage on the other side, crushing blocks in his bare hands as if they were made of paper in order to reach his destination. Looking down at his mighty clawed hands, Xa-Tul marveled at his strength. The memories from the zombies within him had never seen anything like that.

Interesting, Xa-Tul thought. *This strength will prove convenient when I face that cowardly User-that-is-not-a-user.*

He laughed an evil, maniacal laugh. And then he felt it . . . heat . . . luscious, smoky heat from lava. Smashing another stone and dirt wall, he found himself looking down onto a massive lava lake, a waterfall at one end.

That was where he needed to go.

Walking along the edge of the lake, he followed its perimeter until he came to the splashing waterfall. Spray from the plummeting flow spattered on his boxy face and cooled his skin a little, canceling out some of the blazing heat from the lava . . .

"How can the Overworlders stand this," Xa-Tul said as he waded through the cool, fresh water to get to the secret entrance.

His clawed feet slipped on the wet obsidian and cobblestone that was always present at the meeting of lava and water. Extending his claw downward, his feet gripped the stone as he moved through the watery flow to get to the other side of the tunnel. On the opposite wall, Xa-Tul could see a flat section of stone that stretched off in both directions. A single block protruding from the surface and looking out of place. Pressing the stone block, the doors to the Zombie-town slid open, revealing a long dark tunnel. Stepping into the darkness, he heard the doors close behind him, hiding the entrance and the existence of the town from any random user or NPC that might be moving through the subterranean passage.

Moving quickly, Xa-Tul strode through the tunnel as if he owned it. The clinking of his iron chain mail filled the tunnel with a delicate sprinkling of music, sounding like wind chimes as he plunged down the tunnel; it sounded out of place. Occasionally, he could feel his green bald head scraping up against the rocky ceiling, the height of the space not designed from someone as big and menacing as himself. Smashing the occasional offending block in the ceiling with his massive fist, he opened the space a little to fit his needs; Xa-Tul refused to be seen stooping or bending over.

In the distance, he could see light at the end of the tunnel, a greenish glow from the HP fountains that he knew would be in the village; they were always in the zombie-towns. As he reached the end of the tunnel, Xa-Tul stood and looked across the cavern. It was a gigantic, hollowed out section within Minecraft with a high rocky ceiling that likely stretched up at least thirty blocks if not more. The walls and floors were uneven and jagged as if a group of careless miners had excavated the area without any care for those that would be living in the space. Positioned throughout the chamber, were HP fountains embedded in the walls and floor, the sparkling flows lighting the area with an alien-like emerald glow. It was just how the collective memories within Xa-Tul's mind told him it would be. Groups of zombies stood under the fountains being bathed in the greenish light, sparks of healing HP nourishing the creatures. The sparkling embers splashed down like water, collecting on the ground for just an instant until they disappeared. This was how the zombies fed, by standing under the fountain and replenishing their HP. If they were too long from zombie-town and the HP fountains, then they would die, for zombies do not eat the flesh of those they destroyed. This was part of the cruel joke from the Creator after the Great Zombie Invasion; his punishment for their race's transgressions. It kept them shackled to their underground prisons and unable to enjoy the freedom of living under the stars. This would change one day . . . he would see to that. But first, Xa-Tul had to bring order to the zombies of Minecraft and unify them into an unstoppable wave of violence that would cleanse the servers of the disgusting NPCs.

The zombies under the nearest fountain did not notice the oversized monster walk by, most of them lost in the bliss of the HP fountain or just oblivious to his passing. Xa-Tul didn't care, he would educate them soon enough.

Moving further into the gigantic cave, the zombie king noticed that this village looked like every other zombie village he'd ever seen. Clusters of shabbily made homes were situated throughout the massive cavern, their positions seemingly random across the rocky floor. There was no sense of streets or avenues to the town, just small boxy homes placed anywhere they would fit. As he moved across the cavern floor, he could see the tunnels off in the distance that led deeper into Minecraft. He knew that these led down to the level of bedrock where the zombie-portals were built. These portals could move zombies from one village to another and from one server to another. In the past, Malacoda, the king of the Nether, had figured out how to access the portal network, and used them in his campaign to bring his Nether-creatures to the Overworld. That had been how the mighty ghast was able to build such a large army and move them to the surface where he could attack the NPCs and kidnap their crafters. Herobrine, the Maker, had explained how Malacoda's arrogance and overconfidence had led to his downfall. The foolish ghast had underestimated both Gameknight999 and Erebus, the king of the endermen. Xa-Tul would not make the same mistake; he would underestimate no one.

Looking away from the tunnels, the gigantic zombie continued through the zig-zag path that wended its way across the cavern floor until it ended at the edge of a large open square in the center of the cavern. It was a gathering place for the zombies of this town, and right now a meeting was taking place. The majority of the town's zombies were standing about, their leader on the raised platform. Xa-Tul didn't bother to listen to the creature; he had no interest in what he was saying. All he cared about was this village's obedience.

Pushing his way through the crowd, Xa-Tul headed straight for the platform. The village leader had clearly seen Xa-Tul, for he stopped talking and quickly put on his golden armor, then stepped back from the ladder that led up to the dais, ready.

Taking a mighty leap, Xa-Tul jumped up the two blocks to the top of the dais, landing with a thunderous crash, his chain mail jingling. Turning, he stood before the zombie leader and glared at him.

"This zombie is named Xa-Tul, the new leader, and has instructions for all of these zombies," Xa-Tul boomed with a scratchy voice.

"This stranger is not the leader here," the zombie leader replied. "This zombie is called Ur-Vil, the leader of this community." Ur-Vil looked up at Xa-Tul's massive size, then swallowed nervously. "Does Xa-Tul challenge for leadership of this zombie-town?"

Before Xa-Tul could answer, Ur-Vil drew his golden sword and attacked. Swinging his shining blade with all his might, he attacked the newcomer with lightning speed. Xa-Tul could see why this creature was their leader; likely all of the challengers had not expected his speed and strength. This was how the leadership of a zombie-town was decided; through battle, but unfortunately for Ur-Vil, Xa-Tul had the strength of five zombies and the speed of ten.

Reaching out with his massive hand, Xa-Tul caught the sword hand of his assailant and stopped the attack, then blasted the soon-to-be-retired leader with a flurry of punches. Wrenching his hand free, Ur-Vil stepped back, then spun to the left and swung his blade at the invader's legs. Xa-Tul, reacting faster than possible for any normal zombie, jumped up over the blade, then came down on just one foot, the other snapping out to hit Ur-Vil hard in the stomach, knocking him onto his back. As his foe scrambled to his feet, Xa-Tul spun and swept his legs out from under him, causing him to fall again, this time flashing red.

Rolling to one side, Ur-Vil climbed shakily to his feet and attacked. But again, Xa-Tul was too fast and easily evaded the golden sword, moving to the side and landing a devastating strike to the golden-clad body, hammering his opponent with a flurry of punches that were so fast that those watching only saw a blur. Ur-Vil flashed red again and again as his HP quickly dropped until he was on the verge of annihilation, then fell to his knees.

"Does Ur-Vil surrender his leadership of this clan?" Xa-Tul growled as he stood over his beaten opponent.

"It is well known that power does not transfer . . . willingly," replied Ur-Vil, his voice solemn.

Xa-Tul nodded understanding. That was not how it was done in zombie-towns; leadership passed from the fallen leader to the victor . . . the destruction of the old was necessary so that the victor could be the new leader. XP *had* to be exchanged, and they all knew that XP could only be transferred through the destruction of one of the combatants.

Reaching down, Xa-Tul picked up Ur-Vil and held him high over his head, the golden sword clattering to the floor. With a howl, he threw Ur-Vil off the dais and to the floor. When his enemy hit the ground, he disappeared with a pop, his armor and XP floating off the ground. Leaping down, Xa-Tul stepped forward as the other zombies backed away and allowed his predecessor's XP to flow into him. He then bent down and picked up the golden sword and helmet.

With the helmet in one hand, he raked his razor-sharp claws across the metal hat, sculpting it into a new shape. As he worked, his hands glowed like those of the Overworld crafters, the powers from the Maker allowing him to change the code of this helmet to something new. When he was done, he placed the helmet on his head. Instead of looking like an armored helmet, it now looked like some kind of evil crown. Gold spikes now ringed his head like massive, unearthly horns from some kind of prehistoric beast. They sparkled in the light of the zombie-town, their pointy tips looking deadly. His kingly crown shone bright.

Stepping back to the raised dais, he leapt up and

turned to face his new subjects.

"It is a dawn of a new age," Xa-Tul boomed. "Zombies on all the servers shall address this zombie as Xa-Tul, the new leader of the zombie race. And as the namesake from ancient history led the zombie people in a great invasion, Xa-Tul will lead the zombies of this age in a new invasion."

The zombies looked at each other, confused. Some of them growled and moaned excitedly, but most were unsure about what was happening. And then suddenly, Herobrine appeared on the stage, materializing right next to Xa-Tul. The massive zombie ignored his Maker and continued.

"The attempt to destroy the Source and escape the confines of Minecraft failed because of the User-that-is-not-a-user." The name of their enemy caused the zombies to all look up at their new leader, an angry scowl on all of their faces. "It is time zombies take revenge on him and take back the land that was denied the monsters of the shadows."

Xa-Tul pointed up to the ceiling, his long black claws reflecting the green light from the HP fountains, making them look as if they were glowing. He then turned his head and looked at Herobrine.

"The Maker, the one that crafted Erebus, the king of the endermen, and Malacoda, the king of the Nether, brought Xa-Tul here to lead the zombie race against the pitiful NPCs of the Overworld. The great zombie army will cause them to suffer and despair as village after village is attacked until the User-that-is-not-a-user comes forward and faces the Maker, Herobrine."

The zombies looked at Herobrine, then brought their dark eyes back to their new king.

"The NPCs will be punished until their cowardly savior comes forward and accepts punishment for defying the will of the Maker. And when the

User-that-is-not-a-user is crawling on hands and knees before Herobrine, begging the zombies to spare the lives of the pathetic NPCs, then Herobrine will take revenge and destroy Gameknight999 forever."

The zombies cheered, their growls of excitement mixed with exuberant moans.

"Seek out the villages of the Overworld and make them suffer," Xa-Tul yelled, his fist held up into the air. "Infect as many as possible so that the zombie army can grow. This invasion will be greater than the zombie forefathers' and show history what a great zombie invasion really looks like. Make the NPCs regret defying the zombie ancestors and banishment to the tunnels and caves. The surface of the Overworld will belong to the zombies again!"

The zombie mob screamed all as one.

"NOW GOOOO!"

And as the zombies headed for the tunnels that led to the surface, Xa-Tul looked over at Herobrine. The shadow-crafter merely nodded his head, his eyes glowing bright, then put a hand up on the zombie king's shoulder. Forming a doorway that led to the next zombie-town, the duo disappeared, teleporting to the next zombie village, ready to displace the next leader and spread their seeds of violence.

CHAPTER 11

ONCE MORE UNTO THE BREACH

Gameknight took the stairs two at a time down into the basement, one hand on the stair rail, the other holding onto his bagel firmly. He grabbed it off the kitchen table on the way down, knowing he'd need something to eat after he'd gotten online. It would probably be the only thing he'd eat before lunch, for he expected to continue working on his Minecraft mod for most of the day. But when reached the bottom of the steps, he froze, dropping his bagel to the ground.

Jenny was slumped over the desk, the digitizer glowing angry and bright.

"Oh no . . . " he muttered and streaked to her side.

Pressing his fingers to her wrist, he could feel her pulse. Holding his hand on her back, Tommy could tell that she was breathing, but her breaths were shallow and slow.

Are you OK lil' sis'? he thought.

Then he turned and looked back at the digitizer. She had turned it on and focused it on herself.

"Noooo."

There you go again, acting impulsively.

Turning, he looked at the computer screen. Tommy could see Minecraft on the screen, an image of a zombie girl on the screen, a splash of blue across the right side of her head, just like on his sister's

Minecraft skin.

And then he realized what happened.

He'd left his mod running overnight . . . his zombie mod. It changed the user's skin to that of a zombie skin so that they looked just like one of the decaying creatures, but hid the user's name with a transparent font. Jenny must have used the digitizer and been transported into Minecraft, materializing as a zombie girl.

"I bet she did this so that she could go talk to Crafter," he muttered to himself. "If she goes to the village, they'll kill her, thinking that she's a zombie. I have to get there before she does!"

Pulling another chair up to the desk, he quickly opened a new window on the computer and started Minecraft. Putting on his headset, he positioned the microphone right next to his mount, then logged in as Gameknight999. As the game started, terrible images of what might happen to his sister formed in his head.

"What were you thinking, Jenny?" he said to his unconscious sister. "Once you enter into Minecraft for real, it's no longer just a game. I'd been trying to tell you that!"

He should have figured that she would try something like this. His sister had always charged blindly ahead, doing impulsive things without thinking them through. But Tommy, he was a planner. He mapped out everything, made lists and schedules, and made sure he knew what he was going to do before he started anything. Jenny was the opposite. She did whatever came to her mind at the time the thought materialized. Sometimes he was envious of this, but not right now. She was in serious danger and it fell on the older brother to solve the problem, as always.

Gameknight looked up at the computer screen and could see the Minecraft screen slowly churning away.

"Why can't you go faster?" he said to the computer.

Looking back to his sister, he felt a wave of anger start to boil up within him. It was always his job to look after Jenny when their dad was gone. This last trip had been the longest; he'd been away from home for two weeks now. Tommy was tired of the responsibility, tired of getting Jenny out of trouble at school . . . or on the way home . . . or at the mall . . . or . . . She was always getting into some kind of situation because of her 'act first, think second' attitude. But this time it was different. She wasn't just going to be in trouble . . . she might die, and Tommy wasn't going to let that happen . . . no, Gameknight999 wouldn't let that happen.

Finally, Minecraft finished the startup and his character materialized where he had left it, right behind the walls of the village. As soon as he appeared, Gameknight999 saw NPCs all around the village stop what they were doing and drop the tools they had been holding. Ignoring their questioning looks, he streaked for the watchtower. As he ran, he saw Digger and his children near their home, but ignored them and ran for the tower.

When he reached his destination, he bolted into the room, and quickly broke away the block that covered the secret tunnel. Sliding down the wooden ladder, he reached the bottom and sprinted for the crafting chamber. Ignoring the iron doors, Gameknight pulled out his pick and quickly carved a two-block-high hole in the wall. Shooting past the NPCs clad in iron armor, he ran down to the floor of the crafting chamber and found his friend, Crafter.

"Crafter . . . I need your help," he began. "My sister used the digitizer and came into Minecraft through the Gateway of Light. She's in Minecraft . . . I mean really *in* the game."

Crafter looked back at his friend, a confused look on his face.

"You know, like I did. Her body is back in the physical world, but everything is inside the game. She took the Gateway of Light and now is *inside* the game."

Crafter gave his friend a concerned look, but said nothing.

"And it gets worse . . . she looks just like a zombie and not a user." He paused to let this sink in, then continued. "I think she might be coming here to meet you and Hunter and Stitcher, but if she gets close to the gates, she might be killed." He moved closer and whispered in his boxy ears. "I need your help . . . please."

Crafter looked back at his friend, the realization of what happened and what might happen clearly understood. But then Crafter looked up above Gameknight's head, then brought his blue eyes back to look at Gameknight, a sad look on his face.

"I know that I can't get everyone to help, but if a few of you could . . . "

Crafter took a step closer and nudged his friend, looked up above his head, then glanced back into Gameknight's eyes, shaking his head.

"You're right, she could be anywhere, and a few people won't do any good. I need to do something, but what?"

And then Gameknight understood what he was saying. The NPCs could not help a user; the server thread kept these NPCs from offering any assistance. But he had to do something. He couldn't just let his sister wander around as a zombie until some villagers found her and killed her. Gameknight was sure that Crafter would help him, but it would likely cost him his life, and he didn't want to ask his friend for that kind of sacrifice. But he had to do something.

Why did she have to be so reckless? he thought. *What if she is killed?*

Then the puzzle pieces started to jumble around in his head. There was a solution here, but he couldn't quite see it . . . yet. But he knew that he *had* to figure this out, for Jenny's sake. And then one of the pieces stopped its tumbling and emerged up out of the mist of confusion . . . follow the zombies back to wherever they go during the day . . . yes he might be able to do that, but how could he if he . . . and then the rest of the puzzle formed in his head, all of the parts falling into place.

"Crafter . . . I know what I need to do," Gameknight said excitedly. "Stay here and don't move."

Gameknight then disconnected from the game and took off his headset. Reaching to the phone, he called his friend Shawny that lived down the street. Explaining what had happened, he laid out the plan and the part his friend had to play.

"Tommy, this is crazy," Shawn said.

"I don't have a choice, now get over here as quickly as possible."

"On my way!"

He hung up the phone, then paced back and forth across the floor of the cluttered basement. Occasionally, he glanced at the computer screen, the image of his sister as a zombie frozen on the monitor. He had to help her . . . this was his fault. She was his responsibility and he had take care of her, after all there was nobody else that could help. His mom couldn't help and his dad was off somewhere trying to sell one of his inventions. Tommy wished his dad was around more. He started to resent all of his inventions . . . they were continually taking his dad away from their family . . . from him. Tommy knew that he was doing what he needed to do, for the sake of their family, but still he wished he was home more.

Glancing around at all the failed attempts at invention success, Tommy wanted to knock some of them over. Maybe if he broke some, his dad would come home to fix them, but of course he knew this was ridiculous. This was Tommy's problem and he would solve it one way or another.

Looking to the glowing digitizer, he became angry. *What was she thinking?* he thought.

Grabbing the tripod, he moved the device, aiming it away from his sister and to another spot in the basement. He didn't like it still pointing at her.

Just then, he heard the back door open, a pair of small feet running across the floor. Then the sound of Nikes coming down the basement steps echoed through the basement. Glancing toward the stairs, Tommy saw his friend Shawn come thundering down the steps.

"Shawn, over here," Tommy yelled.

Shawn immediately ran toward him, a bag of stuff under one arm.

"You have everything I told you to bring?" Tommy asked.

"Yep," Shawn replied. "I put the sign on the basement door saying that the three of us are recording Minecraft videos."

"Good, that should keep my mom from interrupting us until I can get Jenny out of the game," Tommy replied. "Are you ready?"

"Are you sure this is a good idea?" Shawny asked. "It seems kind of…ahh…"pid…crazy…reckless?"Tommy suggested.

"Ahh . . . yeah, all of those."

"Well, I have no choice. My sister is more important, and I have to make sure she's alright."

"OK," Shawny said. "Let's do this."

"Good. You go over there, and I'll sit here," Tommy said.

Shawn moved to his position, then pulled out his laptop and turned it on.

"I'll watch things from here," he said, gesturing to the laptop.

"Good," Tommy replied.

"OK, ready?"

Shawn nodded.

"Set?"

Shawn checked the controls, then nodded again.

"Let's do this . . . throw the switch."

With a look of trepidation on his face, Shawny pushed the button.

A buzzing sound suddenly filled the room as if they were inside a hive of angry hornets. Tommy hated that sound, partially because it reminded him of the last time he'd been stung by a bee, but also because he knew what was coming next. Turning to look over his shoulder, he gave his friend one last look, and then a shaft of light burst out of the digitizer and enveloped him in a cloud of heat and cold and pain. It felt as if every nerve were on fire yet at the same time he was chilled to the bone. Looking about the room, he could feel things start to spin around him, whirling faster and faster until everything merged into a grey streak of confusion, then started to fade to black.

CHAPTER 12
INTO MINECRAFT
. . . AGAIN

ameknight woke to familiar sounds . . . the mooing of cows, the clucking of chickens and the oinking of pigs. As he sat up, he could see a blocky hill in front of him, a tall outcropping sticking out into open air high overhead. A long stream of water fell from the overhang, pouring down into a boxy pool, the edge draining into an underground cavern. Glancing to the sheer face on the side of the hill, he could see torches set into a dirt wall: his old hidey-hole from when he first came into Minecraft.

Yep, I'm definitely in Minecraft again.

Looking up into the sky he checked the position of the sun. He had to get to Crafter's village before dark. He had hoped that he would spawn back in the crafting chamber, but apparently this is where you appear when you travel through the Gateway of Light. Glancing at the sun again, he figured that he just barely had enough time.

Drawing his sword, he sprinted toward the village with all his speed. Instantly, he attracted the attention of a giant spider. The black fuzzy creature jumped out from behind a tree and attacked, its wicked curved claws reaching out for Gameknight's flesh. Stepping to the side, he moved just out of range, then leapt forward, striking at the spider with lightning speed. The monster groaned as his shining blade sank into dark flesh. It moved back cautiously, the dark mandibles clicking together wildly. And then suddenly there was another spider, the creature likely responding to its companion's call.

I don't have time for this!

Leaping forward, Gameknight999 screamed as he fell on the first spider with a flurry of attacks, his sword slashing at legs, then stabbing at shoulders, then piercing the abdomen. Ignoring his companion, Gameknight drove the attack with all strength, looking to eliminate one attacker as quickly as possible. He could feel the other spider slashing at his back, but his diamond armor would give him enough protection . . . for now.

Finally, the first spider expired, its HP exhausted. Turning, he then faced the remaining monster. Seeing his companion's fate made this spider hesitate . . . and that was a mistake, a noob kind of mistake.

You never hesitate in battle. You drive the attack and never give your opponent the chance to even think. It was something some more experienced Minecrafters had taught him years ago . . . OwenTheBanker and Imparfa. They used to be part of the same PvP team, fighting many tournaments together. They were the best, and he sure could use their help right now. He could remember them being there on that hilltop when the NPCs and users had stood in defense of the Source. That had been . . .

Suddenly a dark curved claw reached out at him. He ducked and it narrowly missed his head.

I have to pay attention!

Spinning, he drove his sword into one of the eight arms of the beast, then rolled to the side and attacked from behind. Spinning and slashing, Gameknight slowly whittled down its HP until it disappeared with a pop, leaving behind a spool of silk. Turning, he looked about the landscape for any other attackers; there were none. Collecting the thread (you never knew what you'd need in Minecraft), he continued sprinting for Crafter's village.

As he ran, he noticed zombies collecting in the shadows of the trees, as if waiting for something. Usually, zombies stayed hidden during daylight hours, their flesh bursting into flames if hit by direct sunlight. This had the effect of keeping them out of the way so that people could live their lives without having to worry about being attacked all the time. But at night, that was a different story. At night, the zombies ruled the Overworld, and all a villager could do was stay indoors and hope that they didn't break down your door.

That was before the User-that-is-not-a-user came to Minecraft.

Now, many of the villages were fortified, with NPCs willing to take up a sword or bow to protect their land and their lives. Things had changed dramatically after he'd used his father's digitizer and come into Minecraft; and looking at the zombies that were clustered under a big oak, it looked like they were still changing.

Why are there so many zombies about . . . they hate the sunlight? Why would they hide in the shade of the trees and risk getting hit by sunlight?

Well, as long as they stayed there in the shade and didn't attack him, he was OK . . . for now.

Heading out across the rolling hills, Gameknight moved away from the forest and the zombies. He could still hear their moans as they milled about in the shadows. There must have been a lot of them, for he could easily hear their sorrowful wails from a great distance. This really worried him . . . what was going on?

As he ran, he could see the walls of the village start

to peek over the gentle rolling hills. The cobblestone walls stood out stark and cold against the beautiful green of the grass-covered hills. Looking to the sky, he could see the square face of the sun start to settle down on the horizon. And as the sun shaded the sky soft shades of red, the moans of the zombies grew louder.

Something was going to happen. Were the zombies getting ready for an attack? Why?

As he neared the gates of the village, he paused to dig a three-by-three block hole that was just within range of the archers' bows. He then filled it with water and stacked three blocks of TNT right in the center. Carefully, Gameknight removed the bottom block, so that the top two hovered in the air, just over the pool of water. This was a little contraption that he'd learned from Romantist, a new Minecraft friend. It would be a little surprise for the zombies, if they attacked. Pausing for a moment to appreciate his contraption, he spun and headed for the gates.

As he approached, he could see surprised looks on the square faces of the soldiers that guarded the walls. They all knew who he was, Gameknight999, but were surprised by what they saw . . . no server thread!

Running through the gates, he paused to talk to one of the warriors.

"Have all the archers shoot at those blocks of TNT," Gameknight said. "I have a bad feeling that there is going to be a zombie attack. I hope I'm wrong, because the last thing we need is another war, but if I'm right, this will give the monsters a little surprise."

More NPCs walked up, all of them shocked at Gameknight999. Some of them whispered to each other, but the look of surprise on all their faces was evident.

"You heard me . . . archers cover those TNT

blocks with arrows," he commanded. "And find Hunter . . . we'll need her. NOW GO!"

Not waiting to see if his orders were carried out, he headed straight for the watchtower. Ignoring the questioning stares, he burst into the cobblestone building and headed straight for the secret tunnel. Smashing the block that covered the hidden tunnel, he shot down the tunnel like a meteor plummeting to earth. Streaking through the tunnels, he ran through the circular chamber and bolted down into the crafting chamber. At the center of the chamber stood his friend, Crafter. His big blue eyes looked up at him, then glanced over his head. Stepping forward, his old friend gave him a huge smile.

"Welcome back, User-that-is-not-a-user," Crafter said with a smile and wrapped his small arms around him, giving his friend a warm hug.

Gameknight gave him a hug, then gently pushed him back a step.

"Crafter, I need your help," Gameknight said, his voice thick with tension. "My sister, she . . . "

"Zombies are attacking!" someone shouted from the top of the stairs.

"Again?" Crafter said as he looked for the owner of the voice. "I'm sorry, my friend, but we have to attend to this first. Come on, we could use your help, after all, you don't have a server thread, so now you are one of us."

Without waiting for his reply, Crafter sped up the steps, his black smock swinging back and forth as he ran. The NPCs that were not crafting swords or arrows followed their leader up the steps and to the surface. Sighing, Gameknight drew his sword and followed the stream of NPCs. He didn't want to fight anymore. Not after the Last Battle. There had been too many good

NPCs lost. He felt backed into a corner, but he would die before letting his NPC friends be killed. That old familiar feeling started to percolate through his body, that rush of emotions and uncertainty about what was about to happen . . . it was fear. But pushing aside the thoughts about *what if*, Gameknight gripped his sword firmly and followed his friend into battle, again.

CHAPTER 13

SHOT HEARD 'ROUND MINECRAFT

Gameknight followed the other soldiers to the surface, then sprinted for the walls that surrounded the village. They'd built these walls a long time ago, to defend this village against the ravages of that insanely violent enderman, Erebus. Unfortunately, they still needed these barricades.

Springing to the top of the wall, Gameknight saw a collection of zombies milling about, unsure what to do. He could see that his TNT device was peppered with arrows, their feathery ends sticking out like the quills of a deadly porcupine. He hoped that it would not be needed. Turning to the sounds of many feet from behind, he looked down into the square. Groups of warriors leading horses were moving out into the gravel square, some of them getting mounted; the cavalry was getting ready to charge out and meet this threat.

Something is wrong here, Gameknight thought.

Why would these zombies attack this village? They know that they could never breach the walls. All there is here for them is pain and death. Something must be driving them to do this.

Looking to the west, Gameknight999 could see that the sun was just starting to settle its square face against the horizon. The sky was taking on different shades of crimson and ruby, the eastern sky already showing a sprinkling of stars. Many of the zombies also looked west and saw their mortal enemy setting behind the distant mountains. This allowed more zombies to emerge out of the trees in the distance, their sad moans drifting on the gentle breeze and filling the air with their hunger for violence. These sounds only served to infuriate the defenders on the village wall. They yelled back insults at the decaying creatures, making the zombies moan even louder.

Glancing across the wall, he saw Crafter standing above the gates, a bow in his hand. Moving to his friend, he spoke quietly in his ear.

"Something is wrong here, Crafter. Why would these zombies come here and attack? They know that they cannot breach these walls . . . not without creepers."

"They've been doing this for weeks now," Crafter said. "And we keep pushing back their attacks, but they don't seem to stop."

"Well, rather than just kill them, let's find out what is happening," Gameknight said.

"You want to go out and talk to them?" an angry voice said from behind.

Spinning, he found Hunter standing there, her vibrant red hair blowing gently in the breeze. She had her enchanted bow in her hand, and arrow notched, a look of angry violence on her face. But before he could speak, he heard another voice scream out his name.

"GAMEKNIGHT!"

It was Stitcher.

She pushed through the other warriors, then wrapped her arms around his waist, hugging him tightly.

"You're back!" she said, then looked up at him. "Why? I thought you didn't want to come back into Minecraft . . . you know . . . like this."

She pointed up above his head, indicating the lack of a server thread.

"Well . . . I had to because . . . "

"There's enough time for chit-chat later," Hunter interrupted. "Right now, there are zombies out there that want to break in and kill us all. Let's reminisce later." Hunter looked down at her sister. "Stitcher, where is your bow . . . get it out."

Stitcher looked up at her big sister and sighed, then pulled out her own enchanted bow and notched an arrow.

"No . . . wait. This is all wrong," Gameknight insisted. "There is something going on here that we don't understand."

"All I understand is that there are zombies out there getting ready to attack," Hunter said.

Gameknight could see a scowl grow across her face. She was probably remembering the attack that had destroyed her own village and had killed her parents. A great burning rage lay within her because of that assault and the death of everyone she ever knew. And now, it was as if she looked forward to getting a little revenge for those she lost.

"Well don't attack yet," Gameknight said. "Let me go out and talk to them. We need to find out what they want."

"Talk to them?!" Hunter exclaimed. "They're just a bunch of monsters . . . they aren't people like us . . . They'll kill us all!"

Gameknight ignored her rants and took the steps down to the square. Opening one of the gates, he stepped out onto the open field that sat between the village and the zombies milling about at the edge of the forest. He was scared, and wondered what he was doing, but he knew that violence should not be the first response to a problem. And right now, he needed to defuse the situation so that he could find his sister. Focusing on the *now* he walked straight toward the monsters, thinking about what he would say to their leader rather than focusing on his fear. As he passed the stack of TNT that he had placed, Gameknight could see that there were hundreds of arrows sticking out of it like deadly thorns; the archers had been busy.

Good . . . but I hope we don't need it.

Moving a few steps past the blocks of TNT, Gameknight stopped and stood his ground. Likely, he was out of range from the archers on the walls, and the zombies would know that. Putting away his sword, he took off his diamond helmet and stood there waiting.

The zombies talked to each other, obviously agitated at Gameknight's presence. He could hear their grumbling, animal-like comments to each other, then one of them came forward. As he watched the zombie approach, Gameknight at first thought he looked like any other monster, but as he neared, he could see scars etched across his arms and face. At first he thought they were battle scars, but then he realized that they were claw marks from other zombies . . . curious.

The zombie stopped a few paces from Gameknight.

"What is your name?" the User-that-is-not-a-user asked.

"Ta-Zin," the monster replied.

"Well, Ta-Zin, what is it you want here?"

Gameknight asked.

"These zombies have been commanded to punish the NPCs of the Overworld," Ta-Zin said in a scratchy voice.

"Why?"

"Because it is commanded . . . because that is what zombies do . . . zombies destroy NPCs."

Gameknight paced to the left and right, thinking, then stopped and spoke again.

"Who commanded you to do this thing?"

The zombie just stared at him with his cold, dead eyes, saying nothing.

"Do you fear to tell me, or does your commander fear it to be known?"

"Xa-Tul fears nothing!" the zombie snapped. "These zombies here traveled through the zombie-portals to this server, and now this server will be cleansed."

"But why?" Gameknight asked, taking a step closer. "You cannot survive this battle. Your zombies are outnumbered and you will surely die. Why do you have to do this thing?"

"Because it is for the good of the clan . . . and Xa-Tul commands it." The zombie paused to look more closely at Gameknight, then noticed the letters floating over his head. Glancing up into the air, Ta-Zin saw that he did not have a server thread, and this made the creatures eyes grow wide. "The User-that-is-not-a-user," the zombie raised one of his clawed hands, "Xa-Tul has commanded that . . . "

Just then, a flaming arrow streaked over Gameknight's shoulder and sank into the decaying creature, followed by two more, consuming the creature's HP. Ta-Zin then disappeared, leaving behind three spheres of XP and some rotten zombie flesh. The other zombies all roared, their moans shifting from sorrowful to angry. It was as if Hunter's shot had released all of their rage, and somehow, Gameknight could feel that it was not just released here, but was released across all of the servers on all the server planes within Minecraft.

Looking over his shoulder, he could see Hunter standing on the raised walkway smiling a self-satisfied smile. She then waved at him as if to say 'you're welcome.' And then the dam that held back the violent tide burst. The zombies shuffled toward the village, their angry voices filling the air with hatred and violence. Turning, Gameknight ran back to the village gates.

Mounting the steps quickly, he ascended up to the top of the wall and approached Hunter.

"What did you do that for?" he snapped.

"He was going to attack," Hunter answered. "Didn't you see him raise his fist? He was going to attack you, and because you're an idiot and took off your helmet, I had to protect you from him. I saved your life!"

"He wasn't going to attack me, he was going to tell me what all the zombies were doing here."

"You weren't going to learn anything useful from that monster."

"Oh yeah?" Gameknight answered. "I learned the name of their leader, Xa-Tul."

"What did you say?" Crafter asked, a nervous edge to his voice.

"I said their leader is Xa-Tul," Gameknight answered.

"Maybe we should discuss this later," Stitcher said as she grabbed at Gameknight's arm and turned him so that he could see the approaching mob.

The zombie army had now emerged from the forest. The long shadows from the trees had disappeared as the landscape traversed from dusk to the dark of night.

The NPCs could see that they were likely thirty to forty strong, a big collection of monsters, but nothing compared to the battle-hardened NPCs of this village. As they approached, Gameknight grabbed Hunter's arm and pulled her close.

"Wait until they are around the TNT and then shoot the explosives."

"What good will that do?" she replied. "These monsters are spread out all across the battlefield. The TNT will only do a small amount of damage."

"Just trust me."

"Whatever," she replied, then notched an arrow and took aim.

"Hold your fire, everyone, let them get closer," Gameknight shouted. He then looked down at the cavalry that was collecting near the village gates getting ready to make their charge. "Cavalry, hold for now and wait."

Questioning stares were cast up at him, but he didn't care. Gameknight didn't want to risk their lives if it wasn't necessary.

And then Hunter's enchanted bow released the arrow. The *Flame* enchantment on the bow caused the tip of the arrow to light on fire as it flew through the air. It arched gracefully through the air, then landed down on the blocks of TNT. Instantly they started to blink, then fell into the pool of water that Gameknight had placed beneath them. The hundreds of arrows that the archers had shot into the red and black blocks fell down with the TNT and sat on top of the blinking cubes.

"Really impressive," Hunter chided.

"Just wait," Gameknight replied.

Then the TNT exploded, throwing the arrows high up into the air. The zombies nearest the explosion were damaged by the blast, some of them killed, but most just stood there and watched the arrows as they soared up into the air, darkening the sky. The pointed shafts then fell down like a monsoon, hundreds of arrows falling all over the battlefield, striking zombies with multiple hits at the same time. Most had their HP extinguished in an instant, and a few of the zombies survived the rain of death.

"Now . . . fire," Hunter yelled. "Get the rest of them."

The archers on the walls opened fire, shooting at the few surviving zombies. In minutes, the battle was over, and not a single NPC received even a scratch. The villagers cheered Gameknight, reaffirming the legend that had started to swirl around his name. Hunter patted him on the back, her vicious smile reaching from ear to ear.

"That was great!" she said. "We need to make more of those TNT arrow bombs."

Turning, Hunter headed to Digger and spoke in a low voice. Gameknight could hear her commanding the big NPC to construct more of the arrow bombs all around the village, then returned to his side.

"This was the greatest one-sided battle ever!" she said.

"Battles are never great," Stitcher snapped, "they are only sad."

"Well, in my book, that was pretty great!" the older sister said proudly.

Gameknight, still confused at what the zombie had said, moved off the wall and down into the square. Everyone wanted to pat him on the back, but he ignored their celebration and focused on what he had heard. Suddenly, Crafter was at his side.

"Tell me what the zombie told you . . . about Xa-Tul," Crafter said.

Gameknight turned to him and looked down into his bright blue eyes.

"He said that they had traveled through the zombie-portals to get here, and that Xa-Tul was their leader; I guess that's their zombie king?" He stopped for a moment to think about this, then grabbed Crafter by the shoulder. "You acted like you knew this name?"

"Yes," Crafter said, his voice solemn. "There was once a zombie king by that name, Xa-Tul. He led the zombies in the first great zombie invasion. There were books that describe what happened in those ancient times, before the Joining."

"I remember seeing some books in the stronghold, before we went to the End to fight the Ender Dragon. One of them said something about an invasion, and the other had 'The Joining' written on it."

"These are things in our ancient history that few know anything about. Now, many are just stories made up by NPCs to scare children into doing their chores or making them behave; little is really known other than something important happened a long, long time ago."

"But this can't be the same zombie king, can it?"

"Of course not," Crafter answered.

"Then why are you so concerned?"

"Someone chose that name for the new zombie king. The person that made that choice . . . he is the true threat here." Crafter paused and clasped his hand behind his back and paced back and forth for a bit, processing this information, then stopped and turned to face Gameknight999. "Tell me, why have you come back? I would have thought nothing could get you to leave your home and come back into Minecraft."

"I told you . . . my sister, she took the Gateway of Light. She's here in Minecraft."

"That shouldn't be a problem," Crafter replied. "We can send word out through the minecart network, notifying all of the villages . . . she will be found."

"The problem is that I was running a software mod on my computer, a program that makes you look like a zombie when you log in to Minecraft."

"Why would you create such a thing?" Crafter asked.

Gameknight just looked down at the ground, remaining silent.

"Hmmm . . . that is a problem. If she were found by a villager, they would assume she is a zombie and attack her . . . or worse," Crafter said. "But likely the zombies will find her first. They'll take her to their zombie city."

"Where is that?"

"Somewhere deep underground," Crafter explained. "The Woodcutter twins followed some of the zombies to a cave, but lost them in the tunnels somewhere down near a lake of lava."

"Can you take me there?"

"Of course," Crafter answered, "but to what end? We cannot go into the zombie city and look for her . . . it would be suicide."

"I have an idea," Gameknight said as the puzzle pieces started to tumble around within his head.

CHAPTER 14
MO-NAY

Monet followed Ba-Jin and the other zombies toward the tall rocky cliff. The tall trees, with their interlocking limbs, provided excellent shade for the zombies, letting them relax a bit. Monet could tell by the look of the thick trees and huge mushrooms that grew between the dark trees that this was the roofed forest biome. She's only seen pictures of it on YouTube, and had heard that there were always zombies amidst the tall trees, but now she understood. Somewhere, they had passed from the normal pine forest to this massive, almost prehistoric environment. Monet must have been too busy talking with Ba-Jin to notice the transition.

Ahead, she could see the end of the forest approaching, a set of tall hills visible from between the thick tree trunks. With the steep slopes and severe overhangs, it had to be the extreme hills biome she'd hear of but never seen before. Carved into the base of one of the hills, Monet could see the mouth of a gigantic cave that bore its way into the mountainside; that must be their destination. As the forest thinned near the edge, the older zombies had to move from shade to shade, being careful to avoid stepping out into the sunlight. Following the shade made it like walking through a maze. Occasionally they ran into shadowy dead ends and had to backtrack to find a blissfully dark path that would continue to lead them to the shade of the massive cliff. Monet and Ba-Jin did not have to be as cautious, as zombie children were not susceptible to the burning rays of sunlight. For some reason, they could step out into direct sunlight and feel no ill effects.

As they moved through the forest, Monet took the opportunity to collect flowers that seemed to be growing everywhere throughout the forest. Then she noticed that she felt funny. It was sort of like being hungry, but it felt different. There was no urge to eat, but she was starting to feel weak and empty, her HP diminishing. If she didn't find nourishment soon, she'd be in trouble.

"Why does Mo-Nay collect those flowers?" Ba-Jin asked.

"I think they are pretty," she replied, rubbing her grumbling tummy. "Besides, I can grind them up into dye and use them for painting."

"Painting... pretty... Ba-Jin does not understand."

"Here," Monet said, "let me show you."

Grabbing her hand, she pulled the young zombie to a stop, then knelt on the ground. Pulling out a collection of different colored flowers, she laid them on the ground, then smashed them, rubbing the pedals into a lumpy paste. Continuing to grind the goo, it gradually smoothed out and transformed into a paint-like consistency. Monet then dabbed some of the dye on her hand and painted a streak of color across Ba-Jin's light blue shirt. Getting more paint on her boxy fingers, Monet applied additional streaks of color, creating a curving arc of white that slowly faded to yellow, bright red squares of color along the edge. With a few more dabs of pigment here and there, Monet finished.

"Now you look beautiful," Monet said, a smile on her face.

Ba-Jin tried to look down at her shirt, but could not see the whole effect.

"Come over here to this pool and look at your reflection."

Ba-Jin shuffled a slow zombie walk to the pool and looked down at her watery reflection. Standing there, motionless, she stared down at her reflection, not reacting to what she saw.

"Well . . . what do you think?"

Turning slightly, she gave herself a view of one side, then the other, then knelt down to the water's edge and looked more closely. Slowly, Ba-Jin raised her head and looked up at Monet. A smile gradually spread across her face. Standing, she turned and stared at Monet with a look of wonder in her dark eyes, her toothy smile growing even bigger.

"This is wonderful," the young zombie said, now looking down at her colorful shirt. "Ba-Jin really likes what Mo-Nay did to this shirt. It makes Ba-Jin feel . . . ahh . . . special."

A look of pride came over the zombie's face as she looked down at her shirt that glanced around to see if any of the other zombies noticed. A few of the older monsters glanced at her and had to look twice, surprise showing on their scarred faces.

"Why do you talk that way?" Monet asked.

"What way?" she replied as she moved away from the pool and started following the other zombies again.

"You never use an *I* or *us* or *we*. I've listened to you tell me about your zombie clan, and your home and family, but you talked about everything in the third person. It's almost as if *you* don't exist, only the clan does."

"Everything is for the clan," Ba-Jin said as if reciting a lesson. "Besides, this is the way zombies talk."

"But don't you have parents that care about you more than the clan?"

"Yes, parents care, but everything is done for the

clan, it is the zombie way. The clan always comes first."

"Don't you have things *you* want to do . . . you know, just for you?" Monet asked. "What do *you* like? What do you want to do when you get older?"

"When Ba-Jin is older, Ba-Jin wants a family," she said quietly. "Ba-Jin eventually wants children."

"That's great!"

"But Ba-Jin is afraid."

"Why?" Monet asked.

She moved a little closer and spoke in a whisper.

"Times are dangerous. There is much talk of war again. Would Ba-Jin's children be safe? Ba-Jin wouldn't want any harm to come to the children."

"Of course, every parent would be afraid of that. This is normal."

"But is war normal?" Ba-Jin asked, then looked around quickly as if she thought there might be trouble by asking the question.

"War is never good," Monet said, not bothering to lower her voice. "But if . . . "

Ba-Jin placed a hand on her arm, stopping her from talking. Clearly she was nervous about this topic . . . about questioning the way things were.

"Come," the zombie interrupted, "must catch up with the others."

The zombie reached out and grabbed her hand and ran off. Monet was surprised at how soft and gentle the zombie hand was in her own. It never occurred to her that zombies could be gentle and concerned about their children.

Interesting, she thought.

"Ba-Jin, why were you surprised by my name when we first met?" Monet asked as they scurried to catch up with the others.

"Ba-Jin had never met a child that was a *Mo*," she

answered.

"I don't understand," Monet said as she bent down to pick a bunch of yellow and white flowers. "Can you explain what your name means? We . . . ahh . . . do it differently in my clan."

"OK. The first part of the name signifies the rank of the zombie. The closer one is to the beginning of the alphabet, the lower the rank. The second half of the name is the family name. Ba-Jin's parents all have the second name of Jin. Ba-Jin's father is Sa-Jin, and Ba-Jin's mother is Nu-Jin."

"Ahh . . . I get it." Monet stooped down to pick some purple flowers then moved over to a patch of red. "My name makes me seem like I'm a high rank zombie."

"Of course . . . Mo-Nay must be important in the village."

Monet laughed, drawing the stares of the other zombies as if they had never seen a zombie laugh before. Ba-Jin looked at her, confused.

She was about to explain what was so funny when they reached the tunnel opening. The zombies went in quickly, with Monet following at the end. As they entered the shadowy passage, she could see the other zombies visibly relax. Some of them looked back at the bright light just beyond the cliff's shadow and cringed. The lead zombie then growled something and continued into the tunnel, the rest of the party following behind.

Wending their way through the rocky passages, the zombies headed deeper and deeper underground. They took sharp turns this way and that in a seemingly random pattern, avoiding the dead ends that one typically found in the underground tunnels of Minecraft. The leader seemed to know exactly where he was going, though Monet was already completely lost.

Turning a corner, they came across other creatures of the dark: a group of giant spiders with a bluish cave spider in their midst. Monet thought she could hear them whispering to each other, the sound of their voices almost like the hissing of a snake. The blue cave spider stayed to the back and almost acted as if it was subordinate to the others. She didn't mind that. Monet113 knew that other players feared these smaller spiders, but she did not understand why. Being relatively new to Minecraft, she wasn't fully versed in all the aspects of the game.

As they continued through the rocky passage, they came upon a group of creepers. The mottled green and black creatures were hiding behind large rocky structures, likely hoping to jump out and surprise the unwary user or NPC, but as soon as they saw the zombies, they stepped back, except one. This lone creeper seemed drawn to Monet. It scuttled up to her on its little creeper feet and moved up close. The dark eyes scanned her up and down, its perpetually downturned mouth staying rigid.

The monster looked confused.

Moving closer, it seemed as if the creeper was smelling her, taking in her scent, but seemed puzzled. The mottled-green creature looked up above her head, then back down at her zombie face and sniffed again, confusion filling its dark eyes.

Oh no . . . does it know that I'm not really a zombie? Monet thought.

She tried to reach into her inventory, looking for some kind of weapon to defend herself with, but all she came up with was a fist full of flowers. She had nothing, no sword, no bow . . . only the razor-sharp claws on her fingers.

What am I going to do?

The creeper looked down at the handful of flowers, then back up into her face. It's black eyes seemed to probe the very fabric of her being, looking for some clue to explain its confusion.

And then an adult zombie stepped up to Monet and pushed the creeper away, shooing it as if it were an annoying pet.

"Get lost, creeper," the zombie grumbled as he glanced down at Monet, then turned and continued following his comrades.

As they continued their descent, she could start to feel a heat slowly build, the air gradually filling with smoke and ash. The haze that floated through the dark tunnel made it difficult to see holes in the ground and steps between blocks. The zombie leader slowed down a little as it became more difficult to see, but finally, the passage came to an end on a narrow cliff that sat not more than five blocks above a massive lava lake. The other zombies seemed to smile when they saw the lava, but now it was Monet's turn to cringe.

Moving carefully along the cliff, the party found a set of steps that led down to a rocky patch that bordered the lake. In the distance, a gurgling stream shot out of the stone wall, splashing down onto the edge of the boiling lake, the fiery lava and cool water clashing together to form cobblestone and obsidian. Seeing this, the zombie leader started to move faster, as if sensing that home was near. Wading through the water, the tall zombie pressed on a single stone block that extended out from a flat wall. A click sounded as the block moved in just a bit, then the wall slowly slid open, revealing a shadowy tunnel that stretched off into the darkness. Monet could see that the end of the tunnel was lit, but not the color of torches or lava. Instead, a strange green light splashed across the wall, making it look as if some kind of alien spaceship had landed at the other end of the narrow passage.

The party quickly entered the tunnel, Monet following cautiously. Filled with trepidation, she accidently brushed her hand against the outer stone wall as she entered, leaving behind a faint red smudge. Moving farther into the tunnel, Monet could hear the grinding of stone against stone echoing through the passageway, the rocky doors closing behind them. Turning, she saw just a glimpse of the lava lake as the doors sealed, the orange light slowly being squeezed out until the doors closed all the way, plunging them into an eerie green darkness, the light from the other end of the tunnel faint. Turning, she quickly caught up with the rest of the zombies. The dim lighting made her a little nervous, for Minecraft had a habit of putting nasty little surprises in the shadows, but the zombies ahead of her seemed unconcerned, so she continued forward, following behind Ba-Jin as close as she could.

When they reached the end of the tunnel, the adult zombies seemed jubilant; they were home. Monet could see them now completely relaxed, retracting their claws and releasing all the tension they had in their bodies. She watched the zombies for a moment, then turned and cast her gaze out of the tunnel and across the cavern that opened before them.

She was shocked at what she saw.

A huge cavern sat before her, a zombie village scattered across its rocky floor. Homes of every shape and size were built throughout the chamber, each being made from every kind of block imaginable within Minecraft. It reminded Monet of a colorful quilt, with every color in the rainbow present down there on the cavern floor. She could see blocks of gold ore, iron, coal, stone, dirt, sand; every kind of block in Minecraft was here, sprinkled across the zombie village. In the distance, she could see strange fountain-like things positioned all throughout the town, each one spraying green sparkles high up into the air that lit up the area. Around each was a cluster of zombies standing in the sparkling spray as if they were taking a shower.

Suddenly, a purple cloud appeared near the group, drawing Monet's attention. An enderman stepped out of the lavender mist with a block of dirt in his hand. The dark creature carefully set the block on the ground, then teleported away in another cloud of purple smoke. A nearby zombie ran forward and picked up the block, then took it back to add to their home somewhere in the cavern.

Pulling her eyes from the colorful scene, she continued to follow the party, Ba-Jin waiting for her near the back of the group.

"Come on, Mo-Nay," Ba-Jin said with a tense voice. "We need to get HP, I'm getting low and I bet you are too."

Monet nodded and followed her new friend. She was right, Monet *was* starting to feel weak. Reaching out, Ba-Jin took her hand and led her to one of the many green sparkling fountains that dotted the chamber. They found the one nearest to the cavern entrance, a fountain that was flowing out from a small hole in the cavern wall. With Ba-Jin holding her hand, the two new friends stepped under the sparkling flow of green light. As soon as the green sparks touched her foot, Monet instantly felt rejuvenated, the HP fountain filling her with health. Turning, she looked at Ba-Jin and found the young zombie smiling, her whole being enveloped by the healing forces of the fountain. Stepping all the way into the flow, Monet bathed in the flow of the life-giving fountain, the green sparks dancing around her like little alien fireflies.

"Ba-Jin, what happens if you don't get back to the village in time . . . you know . . . before you get too hungry and . . . "

The girl looked at Monet as if she were from a different planet.

"Well, the zombie would die, of course," Ba-Jin said with a matter-of-fact tone to her voice. "Sometimes that happens, but it's OK if it serves to help the clan. There have been times when zombies went out to harass the enemy, knowing that it would not be possible to make it back to the fountains in time. The only thing that is important is the clan; what happens to the zombie is insignificant."

"How can you say that . . . what happens to you is important!"

"Only if it serves the clan," she said as she turned to move her hand across the block from which the sparkling HP was flowing.

Monet looked at the wall, then pulled out some of the flowers she'd picked. Dropping to one knee, she smashed the flowers until they made a paste-like material, then she used her blocky fingers as a crude brush to apply the colored dye to the wall. With broad swipes of her arm, she painted flowing colors across the stone, filling in grey blocks with different colors from her flowery inventory. As she did this Ba-Jin and the other zombies watched her with amazement. Moving from color to color, Monet added a kaleidoscope of hues around the fountain, mixing as she went so that they gradually faded from one color to the next. Applying some small white squares to the edge of a red swipe, Monet continued her creation, adding more and more color until her artistic flair told her that it was done.

Turning, she looked at Ba-Jin and smiled.

"That's why I picked the flowers," Monet said proudly.

"What did you do?" Ba-Jin said. Her face betrayed her confusion.

"I decided that this wall needed some color . . . a splash of beauty that would remind me of how fantastic it is to be alive."

Stepping back, Monet took in her creation. As she moved back, the blocky shapes took on a form. She had painted a huge mural that depicted a long red flower with a yellow center, splashes of white on the pedals. It was leaning at an angle as if blown by the wind, small green leaves in the background flying through the air on invisible currents.

Monet looked at the other zombies, and became concerned. They were all staring at it, their faces slack as if shocked by what they saw.

"Ba-Jin . . . is it OK? Do you like it?"

"Ahh . . . it is . . . ahh," she struggled for words. "It is the most incredible thing Ba-Jin has ever seen."

Monet smiled.

"How was it that Mo-Nay knew how to do that?" Ba-Jin asked.

"I don't know, it's just something I do. I could teach you later, if you want."

"Yes . . . yes, please."

"OK, what we can do is . . . "

Suddenly, there was an angry moan that echoed throughout the chamber. It pulled the attention of all the zombies nearby from her painting, and caused them to turn and face the center of the chamber. Many of them started to walk off, heading down the path that led to the cavern floor.

"What is it?" Monet asked.

"Assembly," Ba-Jin answered. "All the zombies of

this town are called to meet. There is a gathering at the town square."

"A gathering . . . what does that mean?"

"Something has been decided by the zombie elders. There will be an announcement and orders given to the zombies of this village."

"Orders . . . about what?"

"It is not known, but the zombie leader will inform what must be done. Everything is for the good of the clan."

"For the good of the clan," echoed one of the last zombies to leave the painted fountain, a smile still on its green decaying face.

"For the good of the clan," Monet said softly, a feeling of uneasy trepidation filling her soul.

CHAPTER 15

THE GATHERING

Monet followed Ba-Jin through the confusion of the village. There were no streets and avenues to speak of, just a seemingly random collection of blocky homes that formed the zombie-town. Running to keep up with her new friend, Monet quickly became lost as they followed a zig-zag path that led to the center of the town. At places the path was only one block wide while others offered a four or five-block space between homes. Monet was surprised at the total confusion and complete randomness of the place. But after a bewildering trek of a few minutes, they eventually reached the edge of the central square.

Monet could see numerous HP fountains positioned on the edges of the plaza, some zombies standing under their sparkling emerald glow. But filled in across the open square were a hundred zombies, if not more, all of them facing the speaker. It looked like an ocean of blue, all of their light shirts merging together into a rippling sapphire sea, with dark claws emerging from the surface like menacing little shark fins as zombies raised their pointed hands in support of the speaker. The coloring of the sea was almost perfect, with the identical light blue shirts capping the ocean, the indistinguishable dark blue pants giving an impression of watery depths beneath the clawed surface. The image was burned into Monet's mind; she couldn't wait to get home and draw this scene . . . that is, if she ever did get home.

Maybe using the digitizer wasn't such a good idea, she thought as she looked at all the claws that glistened in the crowd.

At the center of the open area, she could see a raised platform of stone two blocks high, a tall zombie standing atop the dais. His golden armor reflected the green lights of the town and made him appear to almost glow. Shouting out something at the zombie citizens, the shiny zombie seemed agitated and angry, but Monet could not understand what he was saying; they were too far away. Ba-Jin looked at Monet, then down at her shirt. A smile crept back on her face as she looked back up at her new friend, then took her hand and pulled her toward the center of the gathering.

As they moved through the cluster of zombies, Monet saw curious glances cast toward Ba-Jin and her shirt; she was like a newly discovered tropical fish swimming through this blue ocean; a new Darwinian species evolved from her predecessors and ready to be seen. The zombies obviously noticed her top for many of the onlookers smiled at the splashes of color, looks of surprise painted on many decaying faces. Ba-Jin seemed to be beaming; clearly she saw the dark-eyed zombies stare in her direction, and it looked as if this was the first time she had ever been proud of *herself* and not just *for the clan*.

Pushing through the crowd, they moved up near the front, then stopped and listened.

"They called a zombie to talk . . . probably to discuss surrender, then an NPC fired on the zombie . . . fired multiple times. The zombie died right there while talking to their NPC leader."

The zombies in the crowd started to get agitated. The news of this unwarranted attack was making them all mad.

"The zombie did not attack," the leader continued. "They did not slash out with claws at the NPC . . . just talk, that was all that was going on . . . just talk, and the NPCs killed the zombie for no reason!"

The citizens of zombie-town started to growl and moan, their anger about to boil over.

"Who is he?" Monet whispered in Ba-Jin's ear.

"He is the clan leader, Vo-Nas."

"So the zombie mob attacked the village!" Vo-Nas shouted.

The zombies cheered.

"What happened to the village?" someone shouted.

"How many of the NPCs did they destroy?" someone else asked.

Vo-Nas raised his green decaying hands, his long dark claws sparkling in the green light of the HP fountains. A solemn look then came across his monstrous face.

"Only one of the zombies survived," he said, pointing to one of the HP fountains. A zombie near the edge of the square lay on the ground beneath the sparkling fountain, his body still pierced with arrows. "This zombie just barely made it back to zombie-town and one of the fountains." His voice then became quieter, his tone solemn. "All the rest . . . were killed."

Vo-Nas looked across the crowd of monsters, then raised his right hand up high, his razor-sharp claws extended. Others in the crowd followed his lead and also raised their hands, claws extended. Looking around at the clan, Monet saw all of the zombies raise their green hands . . . and then she recognized it, something her brother had described: the salute for the dead. Raising her own hand, she extended her claws outward, joining the salute. The zombies then all tilted their heads back and moaned a sad, sorrowful moan that filled the cavern.

"To those that died for the clan," Vo-Nas said, "the salute of sacrifice is given."

"For the good of the clan," a zombie shouted.

"For the good of the clan," shouted another.

"For the good of the clan . . . for the good of the clan . . . for the good of the clan," the words echoed across the collection of zombies.

Vo-Nas then lowered his hand and glared at the zombie community.

"Revenge must be taken on the NPCs," Vo-Nas shouted, an angry sneer on his face.

"Why?" Monet shouted. "Why must we attack them?"

An uneasy silence filled the room.

"Because the NPCs killed zombies!"

"But weren't the zombies there to attack the NPC village anyway?" Monet said. "What did they expect would happen? The NPCs were likely just defending themselves. Violence is never a solution."

The zombies nearest Monet all moved a few steps

away from her, leaving only Ba-Jin standing next to her.

"There does not need to be a reason to attack the NPCs. Zombies attack the enemy because they are not zombies," Vo-Nas answered. "NPCs do not look like zombies, NPCs do not act like zombies . . . NPCs are different. That's how it has always been in the past and that's how it will be in the future."

"Trees are different than . . . us, but we do not attack them?" Monet replied.

"Why would zombies attack a tree? Trees are not a threat."

"The villagers are not a threat either, they just want to live their lives, like zombies do."

"This is how it has been since there have been zombies and villagers."

"But that doesn't make it right," Monet said. "There should not be a war fought today just because there was one fought yesterday. All creatures want to live their lives, even ones that are different from zombies."

"What is the name of this child?" Vo-Nas barked.

"My name is Monet," she answered.

"Mo-Nay? A Mo? This is hard to believe. Where are Mo-Nay's parents?"

Silence.

"I came from a different . . . town, I am only just a visitor."

"This zombie child speaks differently from other zombies," Vo-Nas accused, his voice sounding suspicious.

"Different is good, that means that there are things that we can learn from each other . . . just like with the villagers."

Vo-Nas jumped down from the central dais and stormed toward Monet.

"This child knows nothing. Zombies and villagers are mortal enemies. Nothing can be learned from NPCs . . . other than death."

"Why are you enemies with them?" Monet asked.

"It is the way it is . . . the way it has always been. It is what the clan needs . . . to destroy the NPCs."

"You mean that zombies must die so that this war can continue. It is a war that has no purpose, and the lives of zombies that will be lost will be for no purpose." She then paused for an instant to think, then smiled and continued. "It does not serve the clan to have zombies die for no reason. It is time for things to change."

"Is this zombie challenging for leadership of this clan?!" Vo-Nas bellowed, his muscular form towering over the small girl.

A tense silence spread across the town square, all of the cold dead eyes focused on Monet. Suddenly, Ba-Jin was at her side, pulling on her arm.

"Quiet, Vo-Nas is becoming upset. It is not good to make the clan leader upset."

Vo-Nas stepped even closer to Monet and glared down at her. She could feel the menacing glare focused down on her and knew that she was close to death. Fear rippled down her spine as she came to the realization that this wasn't just a game . . . it was for real. Rather than continuing the argument, she lowered her gaze to the ground, and took a few steps back.

Vo-Nas smiled.

"Come, Ba-Jin must take Mo-Nay away . . . to the family home," she said softly, pulling on her arm. "Come . . . now, before it is too late. Mo-Nay can rest in Ba-Jin's home tonight."

Ba-Jin pulled her new friend away from the gathering and headed back to the maze of scattered homes. They could hear Vo-Nas continue his campaign of violence, calling for all of the zombies to attack the villagers.

It made Monet sad.

As they wended their way through the collection of homes, Monet noticed that a group of young zombies were following them, a collection of monsters younger and older than them. They tried to remain unseen as they followed Ba-Jin and Monet, but were unsuccessful.

"Violence for the sake of violence solves nothing and only breeds more violence," Monet said.

"What?" Ba-Jin said, but Monet knew that she had heard her . . . and so did the other young zombies that were following them.

"Zombies are on a never ending path. You are consumed with hate for the NPCs, and you don't even know why. Without communication or understanding, the circle of violence will continue to spiral on forever, leading only to death. It makes me sad."

Ba-Jin stopped and turned to look at Monet, the other zombie children stopping as well and moving back into the shadows.

"What Mo-Nay says is dangerous."

"So is war." Monet paused for a moment, then put her green-clawed hand lightly on her friend's shoulder. "But enough talk of war and killing. Come, show me your home."

Ba-Jin smiled, then took Monet by the hand and led her to their stone house, the young zombies following in the shadows, questions about what Monet had said circling between the green youths . . . questions and doubt.

CHAPTER 16

PRICE OF DISOBEDIENCE

Standing at the back of the huge cavern, Herobrine listened to the grumbling speech of Xa-Tul. The zombie king was directing his newly acquired zombie-town, directing the clan like a giant, living weapon at the villages on the surface of the Overworld. He had heard this same speech many times, and didn't need to hear it again.

They'd been taking over zombie-towns all across Minecraft, and putting them all under the command of Xa-Tul. The zombie king had been diligently delivering Herobrine's message of violence to all of their new subjects: attack the NPCs. Herobrine had been training the monsters of the Overworld and the creatures of the Nether to hate the NPCs for a century now, hoping to use them as a tool to get out of the retched servers of Minecraft. All that work was finally paying off.

"I still can't sense Gameknight999," Herobrine muttered to himself. "He couldn't have left Minecraft . . . no . . . that would be impossible. In Minecraft he has power . . . real power, and is important. He can take whatever he wants, for he is the User-that-is-not-a-user . . . king of all these NPCs. What kind of insane person would leave that much power behind? No, he has to be here . . . somewhere."

He paused to look around, seeing if any of the zombies had seen him talking to himself. All of the cold dead eyes in the chamber were focused on

Xa-Tul.

"I'll go to the next server and look for my enemy."

Moving to the edge of the cavern, Herobrine found a tunnel that led down deeper into Minecraft. Walking into the descending passage, he listened to Xa-Tul's growling voice slowly fade away as he followed the twisting shaft into the rocky depths. He knew that Xa-Tul could handle these creatures up there in zombie-town . . . he had crafted him to be able to handle anything. Herobrine had poured every bit of anger and hatred and spite that he possessed into the zombie king, making him the most lethal creature in Minecraft . . . well, except for himself.

Turning the corner, Herobrine found a large room that was dominated by three portals. Each gateway was constructed out of obsidian, the black shining blocks the result of combining boiling lava with cool water. These blocks possessed magical teleportation powers that users had learned could take them to the Nether. What they didn't know was that there were special portals in every zombie-town that could teleport the green decaying monsters from one underground town to the next.

Moving closer to the portals, Herobrine could see that the one that led to the Nether had the normal purple teleportation field filling the obsidian ring, the small lavender particles floating about its edge. But the portal that led to other zombie-towns on this server was instead shaded an alien green color, the same as the HP fountains that were nestled throughout the cavern above. The combination of these two colors shaded the stone walls of the chamber an ugly brownish hue. The same color showed across the third portal. This one was the combination of a green zombie-portal and a purple nether portal. The undulating field that filled this obsidian ring looked like a sparkling film of dirty water, with brown particles floating about near the edge.

This last one was what Herobrine wanted.

Stepping into the brown teleportation field, Herobrine's vision wavered and became distorted as the portal moved his computer code from one IP address to another at the speed of thought. In a second, he materialized in an identical chamber on another server.

Closing his eyes, Herobrine stretched out his senses and listened to the mechanism of Minecraft. Sighing, he opened his eyes again.

The User-that-is-not-a-user was not here.

Where are you, Gameknight999?!

Frustration built within Herobrine, and with it the desire to destroy something. His enemy was out there somewhere, hiding like the cowardly fool that he was.

"I'll find you yet," he yelled to the empty chamber.

Stepping away from the portal, he headed back up the narrow passage and into the main chamber. The zombie-town was filled with the foolish decaying monsters, their moans filling the chamber with sorrowful sounds. Ignoring their questioning stares, Herobrine moved to the raised platform in the center of the chamber. The zombie leader approached him, his golden sword drawn, ready for a challenge. Herobrine glared at the creature, then flared a violent glow in his eyes. The monster stopped approaching and just stood there staring at the shadow-crafter. All monsters knew those glowing eyes belonged to the Maker, the crafter of evil heroes, and this zombie did not want to tangle with him . . . not today . . . not ever. Taking a step back, the zombie sheathed his golden sword and lowered his rotten decaying head.

"Master," the zombie leader grumbled, "are there instructions for these humble servants?"

"Not yet," Herobrine replied, "but soon your new

leader will arrive, and he will deliver my message."

"New leader?" the zombie asked. A look of fear flashed across his cold dead eyes.

Herobrine just smiled.

Gathering his teleportation powers, he disappeared and materialized on the surface of the Overworld. It was mid-morning and the sun was still climbing to its peak, its bright yellow face shining down on the inhabitants of Minecraft. However, there were many zombies milling about in the shadows of the dark oaks that surrounded him. Looking at the terrain, he could see that this was the roofed forest biome. Tall dark oaks stretched up high overhead, their leafy canopy spreading out and connecting with their neighbors and forming a green roof under which the zombie could hide for the burning rays of the sun.

Trees . . . I hate trees, Herobrine thought.

Reaching out, he laid his hand on one of the dark oaks. The glow from his eyes grew brighter as he gathered his crafting powers and wrapped them around the segments of code that governed this tree. Slowly, the green leaves on the branches high over head started to change color. The lush green slowly faded to a pale green, then a brown, then a sickly grey color. Eventually, all the leaves just crumbled and turned to dust, falling about him like the ashes from a raging fire. Herobrine smiled as he felt the tree cringe and suffer at his touch. In seconds, sunlight was streaming through the hole in the green canopy, striking the zombies that were milling about. Those trapped at the center of the field of light burst into flames as the sunlight and blue sky punished the zombies for the transgression committed by their ancestors a hundred years ago. The flaming monsters jumped around like little dancing candles, looking for some water to extinguish the flames, but there was none. In seconds, their HP was consumed and they disappeared with a pop, leaving behind few items.

Herobrine smiled, then walked through the sunlight and back into the shadows as he moved through the dark forest. He didn't need zombies right now; what he needed were the Sisters.

Teleporting through the biome, he found the edge of the dark forest, a savannah biome, the next piece of landscape. Some giant mushrooms stood on the edge of the roofed forest, their red caps standing out in stark contrast to the dark trunks. It seemed an odd combination . . . he always wondered what Notch was thinking when he created this.

Just then, he heard what he was coming here to find: sharp mandibles clicking together nervously. Turning, Herobrine saw a dozen spiders slowly climbing down the tall trunks of the oaks, hoping to surprise this lone traveler. Their eight legs made no sound as they descended, but they couldn't help but to click together their mandibles as they approached. It was what they did when they were excited, or scared, or angry, or happy, or . . . basically they did it all the time.

The largest of the monsters approached slowly while the others moved to surround their next victim.

They have no idea who I am, Herobrine thought. *They will soon be taught.*

And then the lead spider leapt forward, its razor-sharp claws outstretched.

In a single, fluid movement, Herobrine drew his endersword and slashed at the monster as he stepped aside. The spider landed with a thud, flashing bright red. The other spiders stopped their clicking and stepped back a few paces. They were starting to realize this was not just a user out for a stroll.

The large spider turned and looked at him with

its multiple red eyes, each burning with ferocity and hatred. They too had been subtly trained over the last century by Herobrine to hate NPCs and users . . . his whispers in the darkness and voyages through their dreams making them hate their enemies.

The spider hissed something, then attacked again. This time, Herobrine jumped up as the creature streaked by, his endersword slicing into the monster's back as he soared overhead. It flashed bright red again, then turned and backed away. It knew it was near death, and no longer wanted to attack this stranger.

Wise decision . . . I may have use for that one.

Sheathing his blade, Herobrine let his eyes glow bright, casting a harsh, sterile illumination around the cluster of spiders. When they saw the glowing eyes, they all instantly knew who he was and bowed their heads, the wounded spider bowing the lowest.

"Spiders, where is your hive?" Herobrine asked.

None of them spoke up, clearly they were terrified of him.

"I have no time for this . . . speak!"

"Our hive isssss far from here, Maker," the wounded spider said; she must be the leader. "We are traveling through these woodsssss, hunting the NPCsssssss."

"Why are there so few of you out here?"

"The egg hatching isss soon," the spider replied. "The queen hassss the other Sisterssss tending to the hatchery. She did not want to rely just on the Brotherssss to guard and tend to the hatchlingsss alone."

Herobrine nodded. He knew that the term 'Brothers' referred to the cave spiders; all of them were male and the giant black spiders were female. Because they all came from the same queen, they were all related to each other. Typically, it was the job of the Brothers to tend to the eggs and have food ready for them when they hatched. The infant spiders, or hatchlings, liked to eat the moss that could only be found on mossy cobblestone. As a result, cave spiders would seek out dungeons, jungle temples, and the mega Taiga biome to find the green blocks, though the moss in the dungeons seemed to be the best. Herobrine knew this, which was why he started to place treasure chests in these dungeons, to lure the foolish users and make them fight the Brothers. Few users had enough sense to carry milk with them when they explored underground. Thinking about his little prank made him laugh.

But as he looked at this pathetic collection of spiders, his smile slowly faded to an angry scowl.

"I instructed your hive to attack the NPCs and punish them for being alive on my server. Why has your queen disobeyed me?"

"She . . . ahhh . . . the queen felt it more important to tend to the new hatching, so that the hive could grow. That would give more spiderssss to do your biding."

The spider bowed even lower, hoping to not be the recipient of Herobrine's rage.

Growling, he stepped closer to the wounded spider. Reaching down, he slowly lifted its head so that the multiple eyes were looking straight into Herobrine's own glowing pupils.

"You will go back to the hive and deliver my instructions to your queen, personally. The Brothers can handle the hatchlings, as they have for centuries. If I have to come and encourage your queen to obey, then you will likely need a new queen very soon. Is that understood?"

The spider nodded.

"Now go!"

The wounded spider quickly turned and scuttled

off, its bulbous abdomen swaying back and forth as it moved through the forest, the other spiders following close behind.

"Wait!" Herobrine shouted. "The rest of you, come back here . . . you are staying with me. I have a task for you."

The other spiders stopped, then slowly turned around. The eleven remaining spiders moved back to Herobrine, but stopped three blocks away, careful to stay out of range of his endersword.

"Follow me," he growled.

Turning, he headed out of the roofed tree biome and moved into the savannah. As he walked, Herobrine could hear the spiders' nervous clicking, but he did not look back and check on them; he knew that they would follow him.

All across the savannah, he could see the strange, flat-topped acacia trees that covered the landscape. Everywhere, the tall greenish-yellow grass covered the ground. It covered nearly everything and swayed gently in the warm breeze that floated across the land. It would have been a majestically beautiful scene to any NPC or user, but to Herobrine, it looked disgusting. Moving to one of the trees, he held his hand to the dark trunk. After taking a deep breath, his eyes started to glow brighter and brighter, his crafting powers building. The leaves on the flat-topped tree then started to shrivel and fade until they fell to the ground like ash. Herobrine looked up at the treetop and smiled.

"Let's see if you can sense me now, old woman," he said to himself.

With a satisfied smile on his face, he continued his journey. As they walked, a village started to appear from behind a large hill of dirt; that was his destination. From this distance, Herobrine could tell that it was a large village, with many more buildings than was typical, however there was no protective wall ringing the homes.

These NPCs are truly fools, he thought.

As they neared, Herobrine could feel the ground start to shake, as if thunder were rumbling somewhere beneath the surface of Minecraft. And then a flash of sunlight reflected off something shiny, identifying the source; this village had an iron golem. Villages with at least 21 doors and with more than 10 NPCs can have an iron golem spawn within their town. The iron golem will protect the village from invaders and destroy any hostile mobs that are foolish enough to enter. And this village's golem looked strong . . . and angry.

"Perfect," he said to no one.

"What?" asked one of the spiders.

"Nothing."

They continued walking, slowing getting closer to the village. As they approached, Herobrine tried to stay behind the acacia trees as much as possible, sometimes stopping to strip the branches bare with his evil crafting powers. That always seemed to bring a smile to his face. When they were close enough, he stopped and turned to face the spiders.

"You are to go attack that village," Herobrine ordered.

The spiders looked at the village, then back to the Maker.

"But there are many NPCsssss in that village," complained one of the spiders. "They will have swordssss and bowsssss."

Drawing his endersword in a single fluid motion, he struck out at the monster with the smallest of blows. The spider flashed red as its HP dropped one level.

"Your queen had disobeyed my orders and is to be

punished," Herobrine said, then pointed to the largest of the spiders with his dark blade. "You will stay here and watch the others complete my orders, then you will go back to your queen and tell her what has transpired here. She is to understand that disobedience will be severely punished. Is that understood?"

The spider clicked its mandibles together three times then nodded its dark head. He then turned back to the other monsters.

"You others will go forth and attack that village. You are to leave none alive and not to return until your task is complete."

The spiders looked at each other, a look of terror in their eyes.

"If you do not want to do this, then you have another option."

The spiders all looked to him, their faces filled with hope.

Reaching into his inventory he pulled out his ender armor and put it on. The protective black layers seemed to suck the light out of the terrain around him, the tiny purple teleportation particle dancing about as if they were alive.

"If you will not obey my orders and attack that village, then you may fight me. But I must warn you, your suffering at my hand will be great." A wide grin then grew across his face. "Choose."

The spiders looked at Herobrine, then turned and charged toward the village. As soon as they were seen, an alarm was sounded, causing the villagers to put on their armor and grab their weapons. The ground then started to shake as the golem approached the spiders, its metal feet pounding the ground with its mighty weight. Swinging its metallic arms into the air, it hit spider after spider, making them flash red and sending them flying high up into the air. When they hit the ground again, they flashed red again, then disappeared with a pop. They tried their best, but had little chance against an entire village and an iron golem. In the end, all that showed they ever existed on this server plane was a small handful of silk and three balls of glowing XP. Herobrine could see the villagers collect the silk and XP, then go back to their pathetic, mundane lives after the last of the spiders had been destroyed.

Turning, he faced the spider that stood at his side.

"Go and tell your queen that this was the price of her disobedience. Tell her that more will suffer if she does not obey me. Do you understand?"

The spider nervously nodded its large head, the multiple red eyes that dotted its face all filled with fear.

"Then go!"

The spider turned and scuttled away, its large bulbous body swaying to the left and right as it sprinted away from the Maker.

Herobrine could still feel its fear as it ran away from him, and that made him smile. Turning back to the village, he glared at it with a venomous hatred.

These NPCs will be erased from the surface of Minecraft soon enough, he thought. *But first I will find that cowardly User-that-is-not-a-user and make him suffer.*

"You cannot keep hiding forever, Gameknight999," he said to no one . . . to everyone. "I will find you, and make you feel pain like you have never felt. And when your fear reaches its peak, you will take the Gateway of Light to escape me, but I will be there with you. Your own ignorance and cowardice will allow me to escape this prison that I stumbled into."

He then laughed an evil laugh that was filled with

so much malice and hatred that the very trees of this biome wanted to flee.

"Gameknight999," he yelled to the very fabric of Minecraft, "you will be the instrument of destruction that tears apart this world and your own physical world. You cannot escape me."

Before the villagers could react to his voice, he teleported away, materializing in the portal chamber of the nearest zombie-town. Moving to the portal that would take him to the next server, he stepped into the shimmering field. And as his vision wavered, Herobrine had the faintest sensation that Gameknight999 was near. The server on which the User-that-is-not-a-user resided was somewhere near this one!

I'm getting closer to catching you, Herobrine thought as everything went black.

CHAPTER 17
FINDING ZOMBIE-TOWN

The group moved quietly through the woods, approaching the large opening in the sheer cliff wall. They had been hearing zombies everywhere through these woods; the thick leafy canopy overhead provided enough shade for the monsters to be out during the day without bursting into flames. But as they approached the extreme hills ahead, Gameknight999 could hear even more of the monsters moaning from within a large cave dug into the hill. He knew that when the sun set, this forest would be alive with monsters. They had to find Monet before that happened. The problem was that they had to go *into* the cave in order to find his sister.

Gameknight moved to the edge of the opening, and glanced into its depths. He couldn't see anything, just shadows and darkness.

"We have to go in," he whispered to Crafter. "Are you sure that this leads to their village?"

"These two woodcutters followed them, isn't that right?" Crafter said.

Two NPCs that had accompanied them both nodded their heads. These two were both woodcutters, so they had the same name, Woodcutter, which was confusing for Gameknight at times, though somehow the NPCs always seemed to know who was who. They both wore the traditional garb of a woodcutter, red smock with a brown stripe down the center. Out in the open, in bright sunlight, they made an attractive target for skeletons; and a few had tried their archery skills from the shadows as they traveled to this cave, but Hunter had quickly silenced their bows with her own. The Woodcutters reminded Gameknight of the old *Star Trek* episodes when Captain Kirk would go to some alien planet. The red-shirted security guards never fared well on these adventures. He hoped these Woodcutters wouldn't meet the same fate.

"OK, let's go in," Gameknight said, then darted into the cave.

Extending all of his senses out into the shadows, he moved cautiously through the cave, looking behind blocks and inside holes for clawed surprises . . . so far they saw none.

"Come on," the User-that-is-not-a-user said.

Gripping his sword firmly, he moved through the tunnel, his friends following behind in a single-file line. His enchanted sword cast an iridescent blue glow on the stone walls, adding some light to the darkness, but still it was difficult to see far ahead. Gameknight knew that Hunter was right behind him, her arrows hungry for monster-flesh. He was still shocked at the raw anger she still felt toward the monsters. They had taken her family and friends from her, but her anger was more than that. It was to the point of being an irrational obsession, as if she wanted the monsters dead because they were just different from NPCs. Gameknight thought that she might kill any monster just for being alive, their difference enough excuse to exterminate them. It worried him. Killing should be hard; it should come about after much consideration and be needed to protect your own life. But with Hunter, it seemed that she wanted the monsters dead because they were monsters, and no other reason. That worried Gameknight999.

"There is nothing similar between us and them," she had said while they were walking through the woods. "They should be destroyed."

"But to hate them because they are different serves no purpose," Gameknight had objected. "It only causes more violence."

"They tried to break free of Minecraft and destroy your sister and parents," she snapped. "Tell it to your parents . . . I can't tell it to mine, they killed my parents, remember."

"But these aren't the zombies that killed your parents," he had replied. "They are on another server somewhere else in Minecraft."

"I don't care," she had replied. "Zombies are not NPCs . . . they are different . . . they are dangerous . . . they should be erased from the face of Minecraft!"

Suddenly, a clicking sound echoed through the tunnel, bringing Gameknight back to the present, then more clicking . . . spiders. Gameknight turned to warn Hunter, but she wasn't there. He could hear her footsteps already echoing through the tunnel, running ahead to challenge the monsters. Gripping his sword firmly, he ran after her, Crafter and the Woodcutters following close behind.

Thrum . . . thrum . . . thrum, her bowstring sang.

"Take that, spider," she hissed.

Gameknight found her standing on top of a block, firing down at the creatures. Running to her side, he slashed at the legs of one of the beasts, its multiple hate-filled eyes glaring at him with savage ferocity. Spinning to dodge a dark curved claw, he struck at the monster's back, then rolled away as another spider joined the battle. As he fought, he saw Crafter swinging his own diamond sword, driving a monster back. The Woodcutters then jumped forward, both landing between the creatures and attacking from the side, their razor-sharp axes slicing through the air with lethal accuracy. Two more spiders now emerged from the shadows, four in total.

"Behind you!" Gameknight shouted to Woodcutter.

The NPC turned, swinging his axe as Gameknight had taught him to protect his back. The razor-sharp edge found flesh and tore into the monster, making it flash red. Swinging his axe again and again, he drove the attack home, not giving the spider a chance to escape. And then there was a pop; the spider disappeared, its HP consumed. Its dark companion then attacked Woodcutter, delivering some savage blows to the NPC. Gameknight jumped forward and attacked the monster from behind as Hunter and Crafter took care of the other two. The other Woodcutter was suddenly at his side, both of them hitting the black fuzzy spider with a flurry of attacks as their friend backed up and defended himself. Pop! . . . silk thread; the spider disappeared.

Turning to see who needed help, Gameknight saw Crafter dodging and then attacking the spider before him, his diamond sword a blur . . . the creature expired . . . more silk thread. The last one jumped up at Hunter, but her pointed arrows never let the creature come close.

Finally the last spider disappeared, Hunter's arrows consuming the last of its HP. They were safe again.

Gameknight growled as he spun around, looking for threats. The sound caused Hunter's bow to swivel toward him, then aim downward as she recognized her friend.

What are we doing down here? he thought. *This is going to get one of my friends killed! Why did you have to do this, Jenny? You act without thinking, without fear and take these ridiculous risks, and then make me clean up after you . . . like always. I hate being responsible for you when Dad is away.*

Frustration boiled up within Gameknight999, but then evaporated away when he thought about the danger his sister was in, and he started to shake. He could tell that his fear showed on his face because Hunter lowered her bow and came to his side.

"You're worried about her?" she asked.

Gameknight nodded.

"Don't worry, you took care of my sister when I had been captured by those two monsters, Erebus and Malacoda. Now it's my turn to take care of yours." She placed a gentle hand on his shoulder. "We'll make sure she gets back safe . . . I promise."

"Thank you," Gameknight replied, feeling surprisingly reassured.

"That had been close," Crafter said, "too close. We can't just go walking around down here; there could be monsters around every corner. We'll never make it to their zombie-town this way."

Just then a sorrowful moan floated through the

tunnel from far away; a zombie was somewhere in the underground warren, thankfully not close, but still present. It gave all of them chills knowing that the green monsters could be around the next corner. And as the zombie's wail echoed through the tunnel, the puzzle pieces started tumbling in Gameknight's head. As the moan faded away, one of the pieces clicked into place.

"You're right, Crafter," Gameknight answered, a mischievous smirk on his square face. "I have a plan, but you aren't going to like it."

Crafter frowned.

"By the look on your face, I think you're right," Crafter said.

"I like it already," Hunter added with a smile.

"First, I need a strip of cloth from one of your smocks," Gameknight explained.

Crafter pulled out a set of shears from his inventory and clipped off the hem of his smock, then handed the black cloth to Gameknight.

"Were you planning on shearing some sheep on this adventure, Crafter?" Hunter asked.

"My Great Great Uncle Baker used to say, 'A good pair of shears can be used for lots of things . . . don't go anywhere without them.'"

"Please tell me that's the end of the story," Hunter said with a smile.

"This time, my story is short," Crafter replied.

"That's a nice change," one of the Woodcutters said, laughing.

"OK, look at me," Gameknight said. He then tied the strip of cloth across his forehead, the loose ends hanging down his back. "You can recognize me by this headband. Don't shoot me . . . look for the head band, especially you, Hunter."

"What are you talking about?" she asked.

"Just don't shoot me," he repeated.

Closing his eyes, he reached out with his mind and imagined that he was texting to Shawny. He knew that his friend would be monitoring what they were doing, likely watching it on the monitor.

Shawny, turn on the zombie mod on my computer, he thought, forcing the words to the screen with his will. *Just hit Alt-Z.*

Suddenly, a glow of light started to form around his body, filling the cave with brilliant illumination, forcing his companions to look away. As the blazing glow started to fade, his friends looked back, and before them they found a green decaying zombie, a black headband tied around its bald head.

Gameknight could hear Hunter's bow creak as she notched an arrow and pulled it back.

"I said don't shoot," the User-that-is-not-a-user shouted. "It's me, Gameknight999."

Holding his clawed hand up to show he had no weapon, Gameknight turned to face away from his friends, his undefended back facing them.

"It's me. Hunter put down your bow."

"What's going on?" she said, her voice sounding confused.

"Gameknight is that really you?" Crafter asked.

"Of course it is . . . look at the headband," the zombie growled . . . the monster's voice making Crafter draw his blade. "Would all of you put away your weapons; it's me, Gameknight999. I've just changed my outer appearance."

Crafter slowly walked forward, his blue eyes watching the zombie before him very carefully, his sword ready to swing down on the creature.

"Gameknight?"

"Yes . . . it's me," Gameknight999 answered, and then he laughed. "I said you wouldn't like this solution very much. All I did was change my Minecraft skin, it's still me in here."

"No, Gameknight, you did more," Crafter explained. "You see, villagers can sense when a zombie is around . . . we can feel them. They have been our mortal enemies for so long that we've developed a sensitivity to them. Maybe it's their smell, which, by the way . . . you stink, or maybe it's something in Minecraft. Nobody really knows, but we all can *feel* when a zombie is near . . . and we can *feel* you."

"Feel me?"

"Yep," Hunter added. "As always, you did something idiotic and didn't even know it." She then laughed. "I love it!"

Crafter reluctantly nodded.

"You didn't just change your skin," Crafter continued, "you changed your very being. This isn't just a disguise . . . you are really and truly a zombie. Look at your claws, they stick out beyond your fingers . . . how could a new skin do that? And I bet if you start to walk, your arms will come up."

"No, you're wrong," Gameknight said, stepping forward, then stopped talking as his arms automatically moved up and extended in front of him.

"You see," Crafter added. "That is how zombies walk . . . at least outside of their village . . . inside it, who knows."

"We'll know soon enough," Hunter said with a sneer. "Let's get this party going."

Gameknight nodded.

"Here's the plan; I'm going to walk out in front, following the trail to where ever these zombies go. If I see any other monsters, I will moan twice, warning you . . . got it?"

They all drew their weapons and nodded . . . Hunter smiling.

Turning, Gameknight continued through the tunnel, heading deeper into Minecraft. They came across two groups of spiders as they moved through the shadows. His moaning calls made the battles very one-sided, the NPCs attacking from the front while Gameknight's claws attacked from behind. The spiders didn't know what to make of the attacking zombie, and had little time to do anything about it. But as they moved deeper into the subterranean passages, they faced more monsters, and more monsters meant more killing. With every battle, Gameknight seemed to get angrier with his sister. Her careless, impulsive decision to come into Minecraft had put him and his friends at risk. Some of them *might* die to save her, and she had no idea. It was typical of her; act first, think second.

I'm so tired of cleaning up after your messes, Jenny, he thought.

Sighing, he continued along the rocky path. But as they moved deeper into the tunnels, the temperature started to rise, the air filling with smoke. Gameknight knew that they were getting close to lava and knew that they had to be careful; trying to swim in lava was never a good idea. The walls of the tunnel started to brighten as the temperature climbed until the passage opened to a large lake of molten stone, the passageway ending five blocks above. He could see a narrow ledge that led around the boundary of the lake and followed it, keeping his back pressed against the wall so that he wouldn't accidently fall down into the boiling mass of heat and flame; his arms still stuck foolishly straight out in front of him.

Eventually he came to a set of steps that led down to the lake's edge. Moving quickly down, Gameknight was glad to get away from the boiling pool of molten stone. In the distance, he could see a stream of water that was falling down from a hole in a wall, the watery flow meeting the lava and forming blocks of cobblestone and obsidian. Standing there, looking down at the clash of fire and water, Gameknight was uncertain what to do. All around him was stone, water and lava, and no zombie-town; but this was where the tunnel had led. There was nowhere else to go.

Frustrated about being lost and angry about his sister pulling him to this place, he moved to a block of stone and sat. Quickly, he was joined by Crafter, Hunter, and the Woodcutters.

"Where now?" Hunter asked. "Where is this zombie-town?"

"I don't know," Gameknight answered.

Think . . . think . . . think, what would Monet113 do? Gameknight thought. *She loves art and color, her favorite things. She would want to paint these walls, no, every wall. Monet always needed to paint every empty canvas she came across, and all these stone walls would look like canvasses to her.*

"Color . . . look for color on the walls," Gameknight said to his friends.

"What are you talking about?" Hunter asked.

"Just look for colors . . . you know, blotches of paint on the walls. My sister is messy and always has paint on her hands; she'll leave a smudge or streak somewhere . . . she always does." Gameknight stood up and felt excited . . . they had a plan. "Search the walls."

They started at the edge of the lava lake. Gameknight and Crafter were on one wall, Hunter and the Woodcutters on the others. They moved across the walls, blocky hands sliding across the rocky surfaces, but when they came to a large flat part, Gameknight stopped.

"A torch . . . I need a torch."

One of the Woodcutters pulled out a torch and held it near the wall. And there it was, the faintest splash of color: a small square of red paint.

"Here it is," Gameknight said, his dark zombie eyes growing wide with excitement. "This must be the entrance to zombie-town."

"Excellent," Hunter said as she pulled out a diamond pickaxe. "Let's knock and see if there is anyone home."

"No!" Crafter snapped. "We have to be quiet and smart. Having an entire village of zombies attacking us would be too much to battle."

"Maybe you could use your shears to protect us," Hunter said with a smile.

Crafter smiled back.

"There must be a switch somewhere," Gameknight said, then saw the lone block sticking out of the flat wall.

Moving his clawed hand to the block, he pressed it with all his might. The faintest of clicks sounded in the chamber, echoing off the wall. Before any of them could react, the stone walls started to slide open, revealing a long dark tunnel, the end lit with an eerie green light.

"Quickly," Gameknight said as he led the way into the tunnel, his friends following.

They streaked through the rocky passage as the heavy stone doors closed. When they reached the end of the tunnel, they were shocked at what they saw; a huge collection of blocky structures were spread across the floor of a massive cavern, and with the squat homes were a hundred zombies, if not more.

How are we going to find my sister in all this? he thought to himself, and then he noticed all the zombies moving about between the multicolored homes. There were hundreds of them moving from house to house and more coming out of the tunnels at the far end of the chamber.

Turning to look at his friends behind him, he shuddered. They were outnumbered at least a hundred to one . . . this was impossible.

"Now *this* looks like fun," Hunter said with a laugh, then patted Gameknight999 on the shoulder. "Thanks for bring us here . . . this was a *great* idea."

Her sarcasm bit at him like a razor, making him angry . . . and afraid.

"I have to find my sister, somehow, in this village," Gameknight said. "This is too dangerous. All of you should go back. I can do this by myself."

"Yeah . . . right," Hunter replied. "I'm not going to leave you here all by yourself and let you have all the fun. Besides, you'll probably just do something stupid and need me to save you . . . like always. I'm staying."

"Me too," the Woodcutters said in unison.

"We're all in," Crafter said. "Let's do this."

Gameknight turned and looked at his friends through his zombie eyes and was overcome with emotion. He was so grateful that they were here to help him. It was good to have friends.

"OK, then here's what we're going to do."

Gameknight explained his plan as he gazed across the village, and as the pieces of the puzzle came together in his head, he realized how dangerous this would be, and the likelihood of success was so vanishingly small, that they would all likely meet their doom in this zombie-town. But without any other choice, he finished explaining his scheme, then started walking down into zombie-town, his frustration toward his foolish sister growing with every shuffling step.

CHAPTER 18

A STORM ON THE HORIZON

As Monet followed Ba-Jin through the twisted streets of zombie-town, she noticed a collection of zombie children following them. Trying to hide from sight, the youths kept to the shadows, hiding behind stone walls or ducking around corners but staying with them as they headed for Ba-Jin's home. Again, Monet quickly became lost as they moved through the confusing jangle of streets that crisscrossed their way across the cavern floor. But finally, they reached their destination. Leading her in, Ba-Jin opened the door and entered her home, Monet fast on her heels.

"Well, this is it," Ba-Jin said proudly.

Monet looked around and was shocked at the sparse conditions of the structure. It was literally just four walls and a room. The building was made mostly out of stone, but with blocks of mycelium and gravel here and there. And then she realized the significance of these blocks . . . there were only blocks that an enderman could pick up and steal.

That's what brought these materials here, she thought, *endermen. There must be some kind of relationship between the zombies and the tall dark creatures.*

As she scanned the room, Ba-Jin watched her

closely, then spoke.

"Mo-Nay doesn't seem very . . . impressed."

"Well, it is a nice . . . ahh . . . room."

"It's bigger than most in zombie-town," Ba-Jin added proudly.

"I'm sure it is, but it lacks personality."

"What does . . . ahh . . . Mo-Nay mean?"

"Well, a home should represent the kind of person that lives there," Monet said as she walked through the room. She then turned and walked back outside to face the exterior. "You see, you have this great wall here and there is nothing on it. We could cover this with color so that it says something about the beautiful person that lives inside."

Ba-Jin blushed for just an instant, her green cheeks fading to crimson, then looked back to her friend, a look of expectation and excitement on her face. Looking down at her colorful shirt, she smiled, then looked back up at her friend.

"What does Mo-Nay think should be done?" Ba-Jin asked.

"I think we should make this wall look as beautiful as you do," Monet replied. "And we'll need some help!" she shouted.

Some of the zombie children that had been hiding nearby, listening, slowly came out from behind the neighboring house.

"Come all of you," Monet said, "we're going to paint this wall."

Reaching into her inventory, she pulled out the many flowers she had brought with her into zombie-town and put them on the ground. Grabbing a green one, she showed the other zombies how to grind it up into a paste that slowly became runny as it was mixed, then put a streak of color on the wall.

"Each of you take some flowers and then pick a

wall. Choose colors that you like and start painting."

The zombie children looked at each other, uncertain what to do, then one of them bravely stepped forward and grabbed a handful of white flowers and started grinding. This alleviated the fears of the others, letting them all step forward to grab a handful of color. In no time, all four walls were being decorated with stripes of red, spots of green, and splashes of blue as the zombie children expressed their inner emotions for the first time in their lives, the good of the clan set aside for a moment.

"Nice, I like the green and white together," Monet said to one child as she inspected her work. "The contrast between the bright and dark looks wonderful."

The child beamed.

"Oh my, look what you have done," Monet said as she moved to the next wall.

Before her was a multi-shaded wall of red: all of the different hues seen at sunset, a faint line of blue at the top, the smallest taste of the sun's yellow face just disappearing at the bottom.

"This is Da-Ray's favorite time . . . sunset," the young zombie said.

"Da-Ray, you did a fantastic job. It looks so real, I could almost touch it."

Reaching out, Monet put her hand on the wall to touch the warm red sky. As she brought her hand back, she found it had red paint on it. But then, the strangest thing happened; Da-Ray stepped forward, moving closer to Monet. The young zombie looked toward Ba-Jin, then back to Monet, then down to her pale blue shirt.

"Ahh . . . you want a shirt like Ba-Jin's."

The zombie nodded.

Smiling, Monet applied the red dye to her shirt,

putting splashes of green across the sides. Adding some white, she put some pink streaks followed by some blue spots all in a line. Lost in her work, Monet didn't realize that the other zombie children had stopped their painting and had gathered around her, watching her create this work of art.

"There . . . that looks nice," Monet said as she finished. "What do you think?"

Da-Ray looked down at her shirt, then smiled, a look of confidence and pride covering her green face for probably the first time in her life.

The other zombies all moved forward, wanting to be next.

"No, no, no," Monet said, shocking the children. "You don't get it. Artistic creation is something that all of you can do. Pick a partner and decorate each other's shirts just like you did on the wall."

The zombies looked at each other, uncertain, then a giggle of excitement escaped from one of them, releasing an avalanche of creativity. The zombies painted each other with a fevered passion as if they thought this opportunity might somehow escape. They created incredible patterns of colors and shapes on each other, each trying to surpass the other, gigantic toothy smiles showing on all their green faces.

And then suddenly a loud moan filled the air followed by the clanking of something, metal on metal. The zombie children all stopped painting and looked toward the sound, their smiles slowly fading away.

"What is it?" Monet asked.

"Another gathering," said one of the children, her shirt colored with a delicate pattern of greens and yellows, reminding her of the rolling hills outside of Crafter's village, the small yellow squares looking like flowers in the distance. "It is required . . . all zombies must go . . . now."

The children cleaned their hands off on the grassy blocks that spotted the area, they moved off . . . all except for Da-Ray and Ba-Jin.

Da-Ray cleaned her hands and started to walk off, but stopped and turned to face Monet. She looked at the colorful wall, then down at her exquisite shirt and smiled. Looking straight into Monet's dark eyes she took a step closer so that no one would hear her words.

"Mo-Nay, this is a great gift that has been given."

"Oh . . . it's no big deal. I just . . . "

Da-Ray reached out with her clawed hand and settled it gently on Monet's shoulder, then moved a little closer.

"Mo-Nay," she said with a confused look on her face as if she were struggling to find the right words. "Thank . . . ahh . . . you."

She then turned and headed toward the square.

Monet turned and looked at Ba-Jin, shocked.

"Did you hear what she said?" Monet said, excited.

"There is no time," Ba-Jin said, her own face showing confusion at what had just transpired. "Come."

Again, Ba-Jin led her through the tangle of streets as they headed back toward the square. As they walked, they could hear the clash of metal against metal, and then a scream pierced the air, followed by another and another. There was a battle taking place somewhere ahead, and it sounded deadly serious. When the duo finally reached the square, they could see Vo-Nas locked in battle with the biggest zombie either of them had ever seen. The gigantic zombie held a massive golden sword and wore a shimmering crown of gold that looked like a ring of terrible claws encircling his massive head. His iron chain mail sparkled as if covered with the rarest of emeralds, the metallic links reflecting the light of all the HP fountains, making it appear to sparkle. An evil sneer was painted across his boxy face, his large zombie eyes glowing red with ferocity. This gigantic creature was the true definition of a monster.

Swinging his blade with all his might, the huge zombie aimed for the head of Vo-Nas. Ducking under the attack, Vo-Nas spun to the left, hoping to attack the monster's exposed side, but just as the smaller zombie attacked, the larger's sword was there to protect his flank. Moving with lightning speed, the massive zombie brought his sword down onto Vo-Nas, smashing his chest plate and helmet. Then the attacker spun, swinging his blade in a great sweeping arc, cracking Vo-Nas' leggings. Backing up a step, Vo-Nas glanced down at the crowd of zombies that were watching, a look of sad resignation on his scarred face.

Is someone going to help him? Monet thought. *I hate this violence, maybe I should go up and stop this.*

She took a step forward, but Ba-Jin grabbed her arm and held her fast.

"This is how it is done in zombie villages. Ba-Jin would have thought that . . . ahh . . . Mo-Nay would have known this."

"How what is done?"

"Change of leaders . . . it is done through battle," Ba-Jin said as she watched Vo-Nas' futile attempts to delay his fate. "Only the strongest can lead."

"Strength can be measured in many ways," Monet said. "Violence makes a poor yard stick."

Ba-Jin looked toward her friend, confused, then looked back at the battle just as Vo-Nas' HP was finally consumed. Falling to the ground, the late zombie leader disappeared, leaving behind a collection of items and three glowing balls of XP. The new leader stepped forward and allowed the XP to flow into him. He then turned to face the citizens of zombie-town. As he gazed across the town, Monet felt as if he were staring straight at her, trying to pierce the veil of her disguise. Scared, she moved behind Ba-Jin.

"It is a new day for zombies," the new leader boomed. "A great storm is brewing on the horizon, and soon the zombies of Minecraft will take back the Overworld. This zombie has defeated the old leader of zombie-town and has taken leadership. All zombies will call the new leader, Xa-Tul, the king of all zombies. Xa-Tul will lead the zombie people into a new era."

Many of the zombies cheered, then stopped as another figure materialized on the platform, right next to their new king. This creature was dark and menacing, with a look of violence and hatred woven through every aspect of his being. He was shorter than the new zombie leader, but had such a look of power and strength about him that no one doubted his ability to kill every zombie in the cavern if he wanted.

A chill ran over Monet as she looked at the newcomer, his glowing eyes making her want to run away and hide. She knew those eyes . . . those burning hateful eyes. The rumors were true! She was seeing him with her own two eyes.

It was Herobrine.

"Behold, the Maker comes to take the zombie race to . . . "

Herobrine suddenly held one of his hands up into the air to silence the zombie king as his eyes started to glow even brighter.

"He's here . . . I can feel him."

"What?" Xa-Tul asked.

"He's here . . . I can feel him on this server. The User-that-is-not-a-user is here on this server," Herobrine said in a loud voice.

Monet shuddered.

Herobrine is after my brother.

Gathering all of his shadow-crafting powers, Herobrine let out a loud, sorrowful screech that seemed to pierce through the fabric of Minecraft and make all the server planes quake and tremble. Monet reached out and grabbed Ba-Jin's shoulders as the scream tore through her mind, making her head spin. She had to hold on to her friend to keep from falling.

Ba-Jin turned and looked at Monet.

"What was that?"

"I don't know," Monet replied. "But I don't think it's good."

Herobrine then looked up at Xa-Tul, his eyes glowing bright.

"All of the zombie clans, as well as the Sisters on this server will now come here to aid us in the war; I will command it. You know what to do here," Herobrine said to the zombie king in an angry, loud voice. "I will bring our monster friends here to this server from across *all* the server planes. We will have our revenge."

Xa-Tul looked down at Herobrine as the sinister creature disappeared, then turned and glared across the citizens of zombie-town.

Monet looked at Ba-Jin, both of their green faces covered with apprehension and fear.

"Something is going to happen," Monet said, "and I don't think it's going to be good for anyone."

Ba-Jin nodded as Monet turned back to face the zombie king, fear for her brother pounding through her body with every heartbeat.

CHAPTER 19

NEEDLE IN A HAYSTACK

Gameknight's ears rang from the piercing screech.

"What was that?" Crafter asked.

"I don't know," he answered as he shook his head, "but it felt like it shook the very fabric of Minecraft . . . as if it moved through all the server planes."

Hunter grunted. "It was just one of those pathetic animals out there in the cavern."

Gameknight looked at Hunter and sighed. She was so filled with hate toward the zombies that it made him sad. Since their first adventure, Hunter had become more hateful toward the monsters of Minecraft, as if their differences were reason enough to want them destroyed. It was like her hatred was eating her up from the inside, slowly devouring her soul.

"Come on . . . I need to find my sister."

Gameknight headed down the steps and onto the cavern floor. Moving to the first building, he left the others to hide in the shadows. It was a squat dirt house: just four walls and an opening to get in, no door or windows. Looking quickly inside, he saw nothing . . . literally nothing. No furniture, no beds, just a torch on one of the empty walls and a stone floor. Moving quickly, Gameknight headed for the next home. Sprinting as fast as this zombie body could move, he skirted around a pool of lava that was being fed by a stream of molten rock from a hole in the cavern wall. This house looked to be made out of sandstone and was mounted high up on the cavern wall, a ladder heading up to the entrance. Climbing quickly, he poked his head into the pale home . . . it was empty as well.

"Nothing . . . again."

"Where are all the monsters?" Woodcutter asked from the shadows.

Gameknight just shook his green head as he climbed back down, then darted to the next one. This one was made of stone and it sat next to one of the green sparkling fountains that dotted the cavern. As Gameknight came near the house, he felt himself inexplicably drawn to the fountain. Moving to the edge of the fountain, he looked down as some of the sparkling green shards of light fell onto his foot and were instantly absorbed . . . and it felt great! Moving closer, more of the emerald sparks splashed down across his legs and were again absorbed into his flesh. He could feel himself getting stronger. Stepping all he way into the flow of green light, Gameknight closed his eyes and leaned his head back, allowing himself to be bathed in the HP fountain, his body drinking in every bit of the life-sustaining energy.

"What are you doing?" Hunter asked. "You look like an idiot."

Gameknight stood up straight, opened his eyes and stared straight at her. Instantly, she pulled out her bow and drew back an arrow.

"Hunter . . . what are you doing?" Crafter snapped. "That's the User-that-is-not-a-user. Put your weapon down."

Hunter looked over her shoulder at the young crafter then turned back to the zombie before her. Slowly she lowered her bow.

"The way it looked at me . . . "

"You mean *he*," Crafter corrected.

"Ahh . . . yeah, I mean the way he looked at me, I forgot it was Gameknight." Hunter released her grip on the arrow and allowed the bowstring to go slack. "This place gives me the creeps. I wish we could just fill it with TNT and blow it all up."

"Later," Gameknight said as he started to move out of the HP fountain. "First let's find my sister."

"SISTER?" growled a voice from behind the nearby stone house.

Hunter and Crafter quickly hid in the shadows.

A zombie clad in gold armor stepped out from behind the house and moved straight for Gameknight999.

"All zombies should be at the gathering, not feeding in the HP fountain," the zombie said in a low voice. "Na-Sil should report this zombie to the clan leaders. What name is used?"

"Ahh," Gameknight stammered, not sure what zombie names sound like.

Just then, one of the Woodcutters that had been watching the perimeter stepped out from behind one of the buildings into full view of Na-Sil.

"An NPC!" the zombie shouted, then turned to Gameknight999. "Go sound the alarm. Na-Sil will fight this one until others come. Na-Sil serves the clan!"

The zombie then drew his golden sword and approached the Woodcutter, then turned his head and was shocked to see Gameknight still standing there.

"GO!"

Just then, an arrow zipped through the air and sank into Na-Sil's shoulder, right between two plates of armor. The zombie yelled in pain, then backed into the HP fountain.

"Come on, NPC vermin. Na-Sil will destroy all."

Another arrow streaked through the air, this time

hitting the zombie in the leg, but he did not cry out in pain, the HP fountain instantly returning any lost health. Gameknight looked at the fountain, then at the zombie and knew that they'd never be able to defeat this monster here. Drawing up his courage, he moved toward the zombie, his own rotting green hands outstretched, black claws shining bright in the light of the fountain. Grabbing the creature by the shoulders, he sunk his claws into the golden armor and started to push.

"What is being done to Na-Sil?" the monster asked, clearly confused.

Gameknight said nothing, just continued to push the golden zombie out of the HP fountain. Then both Woodcutters ran up, axes held before them. They hacked at the monster as the zombie swung his own golden sword. Focusing on one of the Woodcutters, the zombie threw all his might into his attacks, slashing at the Woodcutter with a ferocity that made the other Woodcutter step back for a moment. With three mighty swings, the Woodcutter disappeared with a pop, leaving behind a pile of armor and items.

"NO!" Gameknight yelled.

Reaching out, he wrapped his arms around the armored zombie's body, pinning the warrior's arms to his body.

"Stop this and fight with Na-Sil," the zombie said, but Gameknight just held tight.

"Now . . . attack," the User-that-is-not-a-user yelled to his friends.

More arrows shot out of the darkness as Hunter slowly whittled away at the zombie's HP, the second Woodcutter swinging his heavy axe into the monster.

"Nooo . . . " Na-Sil pleaded as he glanced over his shoulder at his zombie brother, confusion at this betrayal painted firmly on his decaying face.

Gameknight held on tight.

Then with the punctuation of Hunter's arrow, the life force of the zombie expired. And in that instant, just as life was leaving the zombie's body, Gameknight could somehow feel the fear and despair within the monster. Thoughts of his wife and child filled the monster with sadness as the creature realized that this was the end and he would never see them again. Glancing over his shoulder at Gameknight, the zombie tried to say something, but the last trickle of HP finally left his body, leaving behind a pile of armor and three glowing balls of XP. Bending down to collect the armor, Gameknight could feel the XP flow into his body, making him feel slightly stronger. Putting on the armor, Gameknight felt a momentary sense of guilt. That zombie hadn't hurt anybody, hadn't done anything wrong . . . yet they killed it because it was a zombie. It felt wrong and made him sad.

"What's wrong, Gameknight, why aren't you smiling?" Hunter asked. "We defeated that monster."

Gameknight999 looked at his friend and saw a look of exhilaration on her face, and it made him depressed. She had actually enjoyed destroying that zombie.

"But at what expense?" Gameknight asked. "It cost the lives of two individuals."

"Two?" Hunter asked. "I saw Woodcutter disappear, but what of the other?"

"The zombie. It didn't do anything to deserve being killed," Gameknight explained. "He had a wife and a child, and his last dying thoughts were of his family and the sorrow over never seeing them again."

"It was not a *he*, it was an *it*, and I'm glad that it's dead. But I am sad about Woodcutter."

Slowly, Hunter raised her hand, fingers held out wide. The others in the party did the same, then as one, they clenched their hands into a fist, bowing their heads to remember the fallen. It was the salute for the dead and all NPCs did it when one of their own lost their life.

"He will be missed," Crafter said as he stepped forward. "But we need to continue. We still need to find Gameknight's sister." He turned to Gameknight. "I think its best you put on that armor and take his sword. You might need it . . . after all, you can't just pull out your diamond armor and enchanted diamond sword and have all these monsters still believe you are one of them."

"Well, here's the thing," Gameknight replied. "I can't get to any of my inventory that I had as a user. That diamond armor and my diamond sword are gone, hidden somewhere within the code of Minecraft. I'm glad I have this now, because this gold sword is all I have."

"This keeps getting better and better," Hunter added.

Just then, they heard a cheer erupt from the center of the village. Putting on the rest of the armor, Gameknight moved to the edge of the stone building and peeked around the corner. He could see in the distance a large open area at the center of the cavern, a large collection of zombies milling about.

"Come on, we have to go out there, into that gathering," Gameknight said.

The other NPCs looked around the corner of the building, then quickly moved back.

"You want us to go out there?" Woodcutter asked.

Gameknight ignored the question and just started to walk toward the collection of zombies, but something grabbed his shirt and pulled him back.

Turning, he found Crafter tugging at his shirt sleeve, pulling back behind the building.

"We can't go out there," he said to his friend. "It would be suicide for us."

"You're right," Gameknight agreed. "I'll go."

"But if any of the zombies figure out you aren't one of them," Woodcutter added, "then they will . . . "

He didn't finish the sentence.

"I have to go . . . my sister's out there somewhere and she is my responsibility. I have to look out for her when my dad is away . . . " Gameknight stopped for a moment as he thought about his parents. His mother was likely upstairs cooking something wonderful for breakfast, but his dad was traveling again, always trying to sell his inventions to any company that would listen to him. It seemed he was gone more than he was at home. And when he was gone, Gameknight was the man of the house, and had to make sure that his sister was OK . . . that was his job, his responsibility, and he'd messed that up by letting her get into Minecraft. He always complained to his parents that he wanted to be treated like a big kid and be given more responsibility, but right now, he wished he didn't have any. All he wanted to be right now was a kid . . . not a zombie . . . not the User-that-is-not-a-user . . . just a normal everyday kid who wasn't trapped in Minecraft.

"But how are you going to find her out there?" Hunter asked as she notched an arrow into her bow. "They all look alike . . . ugly and disgusting. You can't tell one filthy zombie from the next."

"I don't know, but I have to try . . . it's my responsibility."

"Then here's what we're going to do," Crafter said. "You go find your sister, and we'll have your escape ready. When you find her, you run straight for the exit. We'll be ready for you . . . and maybe we'll have a few surprises for the zombies."

Gameknight looked at Crafter and saw a mischievous smile creep across his small square face. Looking at Woodcutter and Hunter, he saw looks of determination and confidence mixed with a bit of fear.

Hunter peeked her head around the corner to look at the gathering, then pulled it back quickly.

"This was a *great* idea, coming down here," she said, her voice dripping with sarcasm. She then adjusted her armor and put on an iron helmet. "Let's do this."

Gameknight nodded, then stepped around the corner and headed straight for the largest collection of zombies he'd ever seen.

CHAPTER 20

THE SMALLEST RIPPLE

Gameknight stepped away from the stone and dirt homes and out to the edge of the large open square. Ahead of him he could see hundreds of zombies, their green skin, blue shirts and dark pants all blurring together into a continuous swath of unbroken color. There were at least a hundred zombies all standing together, all listening to the speaker. Looking down on them from a stone platform was another zombie.

Gameknight assumed this one to be their leader. He wore a crown that looked like a ring of deadly sharp claws that stretched up around his head, their razor-sharp golden points sparkling in the light of a nearby

HP fountain. On his body hung ornately woven chain mail that hugged his massive form tightly, allowing his strong muscles to bulge under the armor. It swung ever so slightly as the monster breathed, the tight rings clinking together, sounding like so many coins in a loose pocket.

This zombie was something different. He was clearly larger than the rest, a normal zombie likely only coming up to his shoulders, but that was not what bothered Gameknight999. No, this zombie king had something sinister and evil about him, as if he were made for just one purpose: to destroy others.

Looking at him, Gameknight shuddered. This monster had something that was terrifyingly similar to his old enemy, Erebus, the enderman that Gameknight had destroyed on the steps of the Source when he saved Minecraft and all of his friends. It was as if Erebus and this creature were cut from the same cloth, somehow, or perhaps crafted by the same hands. Thinking about this made him shake with fear.

No, I won't be afraid, he thought. *I have a job to do, and my sister is out there somewhere . . . but where?*

It was impossible to tell one zombie from the next. They all looked identical. But as he looked at those nearest him, Gameknight noticed subtle differences. One had a long scar down one arm, another had scars across a cheek, and another was missing an ear. They all had the look of having gone through some kind of battle, even the young ones.

Would Monet have the same scars?

Moving further into the square, Gameknight scanned the zombies for something that he might recognize, but as he moved closer, the zombie leader's voice filled his ears.

How am I going to find her in all this? he thought.

Then the leader's voice boomed across the square,

filling the chamber with thunderous words.

"When the Maker returns with the zombies from all the other servers, then it will be time to make the NPCs of the Overworld suffer. The pathetic villagers will be taught again why there is fear of the dark, as the zombie race crashes down on their villages."

The zombie king paused for a moment to glare at his subjects, intimidating them with his dark angry eyes. And then Gameknight noticed something about his eyes . . . they seemed to glow. The pitch black of his evil eyes seemed to spread like a halo, forming shadowy fuzzy rings of darkness that made his eyes look like bottomless pits. When they were aimed in his direction, he could feel a hopelessness settle across the zombies in the crowd, quelling any ideas of resistance.

They had no choice but to obey this leader.

His eyes reminded him of something . . . no, someone. They reminded him of his past two enemies, Erebus and Malacoda. All of these evil leaders had something in common; their eyes glowed with a hatred for all living things, and this zombie king, Xa-Tul, was no different.

"The NPCs will be crushed as this second great zombie invasion sweeps across the land," Xa-Tul continued. "And as the leader of the zombie race, Xa-Tul will stand at the front of the charge and punish any NPCs that dare to resist."

The zombies moaned and cheered, their low-pitched growls sounding like a pack of wild voracious animals. But then, a high-pitched voice pierced through the sorrowful moans and cheers.

"BUT WHY?" shouted the lone voice.

The cheering subsided a bit as those near the dissenter seemed shocked into silence.

"What was that?" Xa-Tul growled.

Now the crowd became completely silent. Gameknight could feel the fear in the crowd, not of the lone voice that questioned their king, but of retribution from Xa-Tul.

"I asked why?" the young voice said. "Why must we attack the NPCs?"

An annoyed, frustrated look came across Xa-Tul's face as the words echoed through the cavern. Gameknight knew of only one person that could annoy another with so few words . . . his sister. It had to be Monet113.

"Zombies destroy NPCs because that is how it's always been. NPCs are the mortal enemy of zombies."

"Why?"

What is she doing? Gameknight thought. *She needs to be careful . . . this monster means business.*

Xa-Tul frowned as he scanned the crowd, looking for the malcontent. Gameknight did the same, looking across the collection of zombies for some hint of his sister.

Then he saw it . . . a flash of color in the crowd . . . a splash of yellow and red and blue that seemed completely out of place amidst these rotting monsters. Moving closer, Gameknight could see more colors . . . young zombies with colors painted across their shirts creating a momentary rainbow of hues and shades. And at the center of the colorful storm was a lone zombie child looking defiantly up at Xa-Tul, her hands covered with paint.

That must be her.

Moving closer, he could hear Monet talking back to Xa-Tul.

"Why must zombies and NPCs be mortal enemies?"

Xa-Tul let out a piercing howl that made all the zombies cover their ears.

"Why must Xa-Tul explain to a child . . . it *is* the way it is!"

"Please explain," Monet asked.

Xa-Tul growled again, then spoke slowly . . . dangerously. "Zombies all look alike and live as a clan. NPCs are all different, some living in villages and some living alone. NPCs look different from us and smell different from us. They eat the flesh of animals and plants. Zombies get their HP from the wonderful HP fountains that can be seen all around the cavern. NPCs and Zombies are different on every level."

"Just because they are different doesn't mean they should be destroyed," Monet replied. "Pigs are different from Zombies, does that mean we should wage war on the pigs?"

Xa-Tul growled again. Now his eyes were becoming darker, the fuzzy shadows around his eyes growing spikey and angry.

I have to get to her before she gets this zombie king really mad . . . like Snipes and Brandon at school.

Gameknight started moving through the crowd of zombies, trying to get to his sister without being noticed. Fear started to bubble up through his body: fear for his sister as well as fear of the gigantic zombie king. Moving quicker, he pushed through the zombie crowd, keeping his eyes trained on Xa-Tul.

"The NPCs stopped the first great zombie invasion and exiled the zombie race from the surface of Minecraft. Our punishment was to live underground, linked to the HP fountains for life. It is well known, if a zombie stays away from the fountains for too long, death will follow. So now, zombies are shackled to these fountains, forced into a life underground and denied fresh air. Then zombies were changed so that the sun became deadly, permanently stealing the sky from the zombie race."

"The sky . . . the sky . . . the sky . . . " zombies around Gameknight muttered. He could feel their longing within this zombie body. The sky was a distant memory that all zombies seemed to carry; the joy of gazing up at the deep blue canopy that wrapped Minecraft with its loving embrace was now forbidden to all zombies. The thought of this actually made Gameknight angry, which was strange . . . he was not a zombie, but in this body he still had their distant memories.

"The NPCs are too different for zombies to live with . . . they must be destroyed, and that should be enough for any zombie."

"It's not enough for Ba-Jin," another zombie said as she stepped forward to stand at Monet's side. Gameknight could see that her shirt was one of those that had been decorated with bright colors. And then another colorful zombie moved to stand on the other side of Monet. Then a whole group of zombie children stepped forward, all of them covered with every color imaginable. Gameknight could see many of the adult zombies look at the group of colorful children with a faint smile, their eyes filled with wonder at the colorful spectacle.

"Many have the same question," one of the zombie children said, their voice ringing with confidence and pride. They looked down at their bright colorful shirts and smiled, then looked back up at Xa-Tul.

The zombie king yelled again, this time louder, then jumped off the stone platform. Landing heavily on both feet, his chain mail jingled and clinked like a set of delicate wind chimes. The monstrous king pushed through the zombie crowd to reach the children, the rings of iron adding a melodious tune to the terrifying scene.

Oh no, he's going to do something . . . I have to hurry!

Many of the adults could tell that something bad was about to happen, but none had the confidence to step forward . . . other than those wrapped in color.

Drawing his golden sword, Gameknight pushed through the crowd even faster to get to his sister. Stepping on clawed feet and shoving aside the green monsters, Gameknight moved as fast as he could, but he was still so far away.

Noooo! he screamed within his head. *Noooo!*

"Xa-Tul will not be defied by a child!" the zombie king boomed.

"Why?" Monet said. "Can't this be discussed? Violence against the NPCs will only cause more violence . . . many zombies and NPCs will die."

Gameknight could see Xa-Tul getting closer. He had to get there, quick! Shifting his sword to his left hand, he forced his zombie body to run, pushing aside the other monsters.

"The NPCs are not like zombies . . . they must be destroyed!"

"Because they are different . . . that makes no sense," Monet replied. Gameknight could see some of the zombie adults he was pushing past start to nod their heads, considering her words, but Xa-Tul was getting closer . . . and angrier.

"Xa-Tul will not be questioned!" the zombie king yelled.

The monster was within two steps of his sister . . . he had to move faster. Sprinting, something that this zombie body did not do well, he pushed through the crowd with his sword held up high.

"Why are you afraid to consider another solution other than violence? The zombies of this village deserve an answer," Monet said, but her voice did not have the ring of confidence it had as the start of the exchange. With Xa-Tul approaching, her voice now cracked with fear.

More decaying heads nodded.

"Here is my answer," Xa-Tul boomed, then swung his sword down toward Monet, his razor-sharp blade aimed directly at her head.

CHAPTER 21
ESCAPE

Gameknight's blade made it just in time to catch Xa-Tul's, the two swords crashing together like thunder. His whole body shook with the violent collision of their swords, his arm almost going numb from the strength of the zombie's blow. Xa-Tul was strong, really strong, and Gameknight had just barely been able to stop his gigantic sword from reaching his sister. Looking up into the dark glowing eyes of the zombie king, Gameknight could see a look of surprise on the monster's face, but also a look of unbridled hatred and a thirst for violence. This was a creature designed for inflicting pain and misery, and he'd just redirected his wrath from Monet to himself.

What am I doing?

"What's this?!" he growled as he turned and glared down at Gameknight999.

The other zombies all moved back and gave the combatants more space, none of them wanting to get accidently hit by Xa-Tul's massive sword.

"You dare challenge Xa-Tul?!"

Gameknight said nothing; he just stood his ground. His whole body shook with fear as the monster stared down at him, the blood red pupils like two burning lasers. Xa-Tul growled as he inspected his next victim, and this made Gameknight shake even more. This monster was the biggest thing he'd ever faced, and made the Ender Dragon look like a harmless dragonfly.

Glancing to the side, he could see Monet watching from the edge of the circle, her zombie face creased with fear and confusion. She obviously didn't know who he was yet, but realized that after Xa-Tul was done with him, he would turn his rage on her.

What am I going to do. How do I fight a monster this strong?

Raising his sword high, Xa-Tul started to swing his massive blade again, this time aimed directly at Gameknight999. But as the User-that-is-not-a-user readied himself for another mighty blow, a flaming arrow streaked through the air and hit Xa-Tul in the shoulder, deflecting his swing and causing the sword to be easily deflected.

Hunter! Gameknight thought.

Ignoring Gameknight, the monster looked up to see where the arrow came from. Just then another arrow struck the creature in the back, coming from the other side of the square.

Crafter!

Xa-Tul leaned his head back and howled straight up at the ceiling of the massive cavern, filling the stone chamber with echoes of fury.

"THERE ARE NPCS IN ZOMBIE-TOWN!" Xa-Tul yelled.

This shocked all the zombies into motion. The monsters ran in all directions like an army of startled ants, their moaning bodies brushing past Gameknight and shoving him this way and that.

This is my chance, he thought.

Leaping to the edge of the circle, he reached out and grabbed Monet's arm firmly in his own claw-tipped green hand. Pulling her away from the other colorfully painted zombies, he ran toward the exit. One of the zombies, the one that called herself Ba-Jin, reached out toward Monet, but Gameknight pushed her hand away and ran, drawing Monet with him.

Pushing through the chaotic crowd, they headed for the distant exit that sat high up on the cavern wall. Gameknight could hear Xa-Tul yelling for the zombies to follow, but they didn't understand, they were too scared to do anything but panic.

"NPCs are invading . . . NPCs are invading!" the zombies screamed as they ran about, not knowing what to do.

"Get them . . . attack that zombie!" Xa-Tul yelled as Gameknight ran.

"But zombies don't attack other zombies," he heard a monster reply, "unless challenging for leadership of the clan."

There was a loud crash and a scream as Xa-Tul's blade silenced the monster.

"Now . . . GET THEM OR ELSE!" the zombie king yelled.

This time the zombies responded, all of them growling in unison. Glancing over his shoulder, Gameknight could see the monster horde hot in pursuit, the creatures shuffling forward, their arms held out in front of them.

Thankfully they aren't running, Gameknight thought, *not yet.*

As Gameknight and Monet left the square, he could see barbed shafts streak from somewhere on the rooftops. Their pointed tips sank into the lead zombies; but it did not stem the tide. Xa-Tul's golden sword sliced through the slowest monsters, forcing the rest to move faster to catch their prey. Gameknight could hear the zombie king's low-pitched growls rumbling across the cavern as he screamed for the mob to move quicker.

As Gameknight ran, Monet looked up at him.

"Who are you?" she asked as she looked up at him.

"I'm your brother, Gameknight999, you knucklehead, and I'm here to rescue you."

"Rescue me?" she said, then looked over her shoulder at the army of zombies moving toward them. She then turned and looked back at her brother, a mischievous smile on her green face. "But who's going to rescue you?"

"You're funny," he snapped. "I can't believe you did this . . . used the digitizer. That was foolish. You put yourself in danger, in real danger, and now I have to fix everything . . . like always. What were you thinking?"

"I just wanted to meet your friends," she replied. "I wasn't in much danger until you showed up."

"Are you kidding, that monster was about to kill you!"

"Yeah, that part didn't work out like I planned," she replied.

"Planned . . . since when did you ever plan anything? You just act without thinking! And now we have a zombie army chasing us."

"Well," she replied. "It could be worse."

"Could be worse?!"

Gameknight growled in frustration. Just then, Crafter leapt down from a rooftop, flashing red as he took some damage. He ran in step with the other two.

"Hello, you must be the sister of the

User-that-is-not-a-user," Crafter said. "It is a great honor to finally speak with you."

"Crafter . . . I'm talking with Crafter!" she exclaimed, excitement showing on her zombie face.

He reached over to shake her hand as they ran, but then pulled back as she extended her green-clawed zombie-hand. Crafter looked embarrassed as he glanced down at the offered hand, then hesitantly extended it again. Monet took the hand and shook it happily. Crafter looked down at his hand and was surprised to find it uninjured and unmarred.

"Huh," Crafter said as if he was lost in thought, following Gameknight without thinking, Monet still giggling with excitement.

"I know all about your adventures, Crafter," Monet said, her voice still crackling with excitement as they ran through the narrow streets. "I read through all of my brother's notes. He's going to write a book about it, you know."

"Is that so?" the NPC replied, his unibrow raising on one side.

"Well . . . I was going to tell you about . . . " He then glanced at his sister, an angry scowl on his face. "You're not supposed to go through my stuff, Jenny!"

"Don't use real names online . . . remember," she corrected.

Gameknight frowned, knowing she was right.

"Besides," she continued, "you wouldn't give me all the details, just bits and pieces, so I had to find out for myself." The trio reached the end of a street and turned left around the edge of a dirt-block building. "Have you decided on a title for the first book yet?"

"First book?" Crafter asked.

"Yeah," Monet answered, "he's going to make a book for each world . . . you know, the Overworld, the Nether, and the End."

"Interesting," the NPC replied as he eyed his friend. "A history of the battles to save Minecraft."

"I was going to ask you . . . make sure you were OK with it," Gameknight answered sheepishly as they turned another corner.

As they rounded the corner, they found themselves staring down the shaft of an arrow, the deadly projectile drawn back, ready to be fired.

"It's Hunter . . . yeah!!!" Monet exclaimed.

"What?" Hunter responded.

"Hunter, this is Gameknight's sister, Monet113," Crafter said as he moved closer to Hunter, gently putting a hand on her bow and pulling it down.

"How do you know she's not . . . one of them?"

"I know my own sister," Gameknight replied, then turned and scowled at Monet. "Trust me, nobody can be as annoying as my little sister . . . this is her."

"So you are the one foolish enough to dress up in a zombie costume and come to zombie-town." Hunter said, then turned and glanced at Gameknight999. "You must have learned that from your brother."

"Hunter, not now," Crafter said.

"Is Stitcher here?" Monet asked. "I wanna meet Stitcher . . . I wanna meet Stitcher."

"This isn't a game, girl," Hunter snapped. "I wouldn't bring my sister down here into this terrible place and risk her life by having her near these monsters. It may look like a game to you, but it's life and death for us . . . and death is coming pretty quick, look."

They turned and saw the flood of zombies crash against the buildings of zombie-town, the flow of green bodies slowed by the narrow streets. The sounds of angry moans and enraged growls started to fill the air.

"We have to get out of here," Gameknight said. "Come on!"

He led them away from the angry horde and back

toward the cavern entrance. As he ran, he could hear Xa-Tul yelling at the zombies to run, not shuffle. Some of the zombies then yelled out in pain, the screams stopping only to be replaced with the sounds of running zombie feet; the zombies were now running after them. Glancing over his shoulder, Gameknight confirmed it; the entire mob was now sprinting.

Zigzagging between the buildings, they ran toward the large cavern entrance, but all the buildings looked alike, each made of a different kind of material and haphazardly placed anywhere on the cavern floor. Heading between a sandstone building and one made of stone, Gameknight turned a corner and was suddenly faced with a dead end . . . the path blocked by a stone wall. Turning around, they followed their trail and chose another narrow pathway that snaked its way through the town. Following this past another five buildings, they again came to a dead end . . . they were lost and the sounds of the zombies were getting louder.

"I don't know which way to go!" Gameknight said, his voice cracking with frustration and fear.

"This was a *great* idea coming down here," Hunter added.

"Hunter, not now," Crafter chided.

"The fountains," Monet said softly as she closed her eyes.

"What?" Gameknight asked.

Monet opened her eyes and gave her brother an annoyed look . . . something he was used to getting from her.

"The fountains . . . it's how the zombies feed and what forces them to live here, in this underground cavern." Monet then turned and faced her brother. "Feel for the fountains, all zombies can sense them."

Gameknight gave his sister an eerie toothy smile,

then reached out and rubbed the top of her bald head. Surprisingly, he could feel soft fuzz covering the zombie head, the splash of blue across her scalp feeling the softest.

Hunter launched an arrow high into the air. The shaft arced up then came down somewhere into the zombie village, its landing punctuated with the howl of a monster.

She smiled.

Gameknight shook his head, then closed his eyes and reached out with his senses. Listening to the music of Minecraft, he instantly detected the fountains. They sounded . . . strange . . . like a waterfall of sparkling crystals mixed with the tinkling of wind chimes. Opening his dark eyes, he could now feel the path they needed.

"This way," he said as he ran off, not waiting for the others to follow.

The party swerved through the village, taking a meandering path through the maze of homes and narrow streets, but this time they met no dead ends. In minutes they finally found the edge of the cavern, a set of rough-hewn steps leading upward to the dark entrance. Sprinting up the steps, Gameknight came to the HP fountain that sat near the large tunnel that led out of zombie-town. As he passed, he could feel the splash of green HP sparks dancing around his feet and getting absorbed. It was exhilarating. Instantly, he felt stronger and more alert. Turning, he found Monet standing next to the fountain, looking up at her brother and smiling.

He laughed.

"What's so funny?" snapped Hunter.

"Crafter, come here," Gameknight said. "I saw you take some damage when you jumped off a building."

"Yes, I did take a little."

"Come here, quickly."

Crafter moved to his friends' side and then felt the splash of the sparkling fountain at his feet. Instantly, he felt the flow of HP going into him, healing his injury, causing a smile to grow across his square face, but quickly was replaced by a frown as the growls of the zombies filled the air.

Looking down at the floor of the cavern, Gameknight could see the army of zombies approaching the stairs, their dark eyes filled with malice and hate.

"Anytime you all feeling like running for your lives, let me know," Hunter said. "I'll be out here."

Firing an arrow at the zombie that was at the bottom of the steps, she turned and ran into the tunnel that led to the secret entrance.

"Let's get out of here," Gameknight said as he pushed Monet and Crafter out of the fountain and into the dark tunnel.

Waiting for Monet and Crafter to go ahead of him, Gameknight looked back at the cavern and the monstrous wave of violence that was crashing upon its shore. At the far end of the cavern, he could see dark tunnels that plunged down into the depths of Minecraft, but instead of shadowy passages, he saw a constant flow of green bodies emerging; more zombies were coming from somewhere . . . a lot of them.

This has turned into a full-scale zombie invasion! he thought as he spun and headed for the exit.

As he ran, he could hear the growls and moans of the monsters as they ascended the steps that led to this tunnel. At the far end, he could see his friends waiting for him, their worried faces lit by the light of a redstone torch held in Woodcutter's hand.

"Glad you could join us," Hunter said.

Gameknight smiled and patted his friend on the shoulder.

"Let's go," Crafter said. "Is everyone ready?"

"They're all ready whether they like it or not," Hunter said. "Let's get out of here."

Turning, she ran out of the tunnel and into the underground passage that was lit with lava, the sound of running water nearby. Woodcutter held a redstone torch near the ground, and in the glow of the torch, they could see lines of redstone powder leading to blocks of TNT; they were going to destroy the tunnel.

"NO . . . it will seal them in . . . Ba-Jin!" Monet yelled and moved to go back into the tunnel.

Gameknight grabbed her arm and pulled her away.

"What are you doing? We have to get out of here."

"But the explosives, it will kill zombies . . . maybe my friend."

Hunter heard this and stopped, then spun and yelled from across the lava stream.

"Friend?! Zombies and NPCs can never be friends; they are just too different."

"No," Monet replied, "you're wrong. They are people just like us, with hopes and dreams, and . . . "

"NO . . . they are animals," Hunter snapped, "and they are about to be destroyed. If you want to join them go ahead, but if I were you, I'd get away from the tunnel entrance right now." She turned to Woodcutter. "Do it!"

Woodcutter planted the redstone torch next to a line of powder, then turned and ran. Monet took a step toward the blinking red and black explosives.

"No!" she cried.

Gameknight grabbed his sister and threw her over his shoulder. Running through the gurgling stream, he did not look back, he just ran for his life until they were on the other side of the bubbling lava that met the trickling stream. As he ran he could hear the zombies entering the tunnel, their moans amplified by the cold stone walls. Suddenly, he could feel the blast of the detonation as it tore apart the secret tunnel that led to Zombie-town. The painful screams from monsters punctuated the explosion and echoed through the passage as the blast tore HP from zombie bodies.

"Noooo!" Monet yelled as she looked back at the destruction. "My friends . . . "

Catching up to Hunter and the others, Gameknight stopped running and put Monet on the ground. Turning to look back at the destruction, she took a few steps toward the rubble.

"You can't go down there and help them," Hunter warned. "They will tear you to shreds in seconds. Then you'll see what kind of friends they really are."

Monet stopped, then turned and looked up into Hunter's brown eyes. Moving to his sister's side, Gameknight put an arm around her small zombie shoulders.

"She's right," he said. "We have to get out of here before they regroup and get though all that rubble."

Sighing, Monet nodded and followed the NPCs through the lava-lit passage.

Waiting until all were moving, Gameknight brought up the rear.

We have to get to safety before those zombies catch us, Gameknight thought as he ran. *But where could we be safe?*

He only knew of one place that might be able to stand up against this wave a violence, so he did the only thing he could do right now . . . he ran. As he sprinted away, he could hear Xa-Tul bellowing out his rage. The zombie king's angry growls added to the symphony of sad and angry moans that were coming from the zombie army.

Glancing back over his shoulder, he could see Xa-Tul standing on a block of stone that sat in the middle of the lava lake, his dark eyes glaring at him with hatred, the constant flow of green bodies surging through the tunnels like an unstoppable flood, and at that moment, Gameknight knew that the second great zombie invasion had come to Minecraft.

Closing his eyes for a moment, he thought about his keyboard in the basement and imagined himself typing a careful series of words to his friend.

Shawny, I sure could use some help!

CHAPTER 22
RACE TO SAFETY

They moved through the underground passages as fast as they could, the uneven ground and occasional lava flow making the path at times precarious. The sound of zombie footsteps echoed throughout the tunnels, urging them forward and filling their ears with thunder. Because of the volume, Gameknight couldn't tell how far behind they were, but he knew that it would take time for the monsters to get through the destroyed tunnel.

"Crafter, you have anything for the zombies?" Gameknight asked.

The NPC glanced over his shoulder and smiled.

"You remember what my Great Uncle Weaver told me?" Crafter asked

Gameknight didn't answer, he just nodded to his friend.

"What . . . what?" Monet asked.

"He said that many problems with monsters can

be solved with a little creativity and a lot of TNT," Crafter explained.

Pausing for a moment, Crafter placed some blocks of TNT near a stream of water that was flowing out of a wall. Striking it with his flint and steel, Crafter set the explosive to blinking.

"Run!" he shouted and he sprinted away.

BOOM!!!

The blast opened the wall and allowed more water to flow out, the tiny little stream now a raging river.

"That will slow them a bit," Crafter said.

As they ran, Crafter planted more blocks of TNT where the flat tunnel floor could be changed to a deep, cratered mess, making it difficult for the zombies to traverse. Gameknight knew that it would not stop the monsters, but at least it would slow them a bit.

A few unfortunate spiders poked their multi-eyed faces out of the shadows. The NPCs fell on them with a lethal ferocity, the individual spiders having almost no chance to defend themselves against their attackers. Monet always stayed to the back as the others fought the black fuzzy creatures. Gameknight felt conscious of her presence, and always made sure that he could see her out of the corner of his eye. He had to make sure that she was safe, and that made fighting these monsters that much more difficult. Staying alive himself was hard enough, and now he had to be responsible for someone else as well. He didn't like this responsibility, but knew it was his to shoulder.

As they finished off the last of the eight-legged creatures, Gameknight turned to his sister, his frustration now boiling over.

"I still can't believe you did this," he snapped.

Monet didn't reply; she just hung her head and looked at the ground.

"You are always doing stuff like this when Dad is away, and it falls on me to take care of it. The last time, you made the school bully, Snipes, mad and I had to stop him; my ribs still hurt from that! And before that, you painted our dog, Barky. I ruined my favorite pair of jeans getting him cleaned up. Every time Dad is away you do something. He said that I had to be the man of the house and take care of you, but every time he's gone, it's something else. I'm tired of being the man of the house . . . I just want to be me, I just want to be his son and that's all. Why can't it be like that?"

Monet again stayed silent.

Gameknight turned away and stared at the rocky wall, his anger making him growl.

Just then, the moans of the zombies pursuing them echoed through the tunnel and brought them all back to reality.

"You know, this is fun and all, standing here and having a nice chat, but maybe we should start running for our lives right now," Hunter said with a smile.

"Hunter is right, we must flee," Crafter added.

Gameknight turned his head and glared at his sister, then turned and ran, leading the group through the shadowy passage. As he ran, he could see the walls slowly fade from dark and featureless to something shaded with soft hues of reds and pinks; the reddish glow of sunset was starting to fill the rocky tunnel.

They had reached the surface.

Stepping out into the light, Gameknight was glad to see the sky peaking through the thick foliage of the roofed forest, though it was dusk. Sparkling pinpoints of light were starting to pierce through the veil of the darkening blue eastern sky; night was coming. Looking to the west, he could see the sun's square face from between the thick tree trunks just starting to settle against the horizon. The sky was turning a deep crimson as the white clouds started to blush a beautiful pink. Monet moved next to her brother and looked at the sunset, her dark eyes filled with wonder.

"It's beautiful," she said. "I could stand here and watch this forever."

"There are a great many things within Minecraft that are just as beautiful," Hunter said, "and I would be glad to take you and Stitcher and show them to you." A smile formed on Monet's face. "But first we need to get out of here and figure out how to stop the war that you just started."

Her smile evaporated.

"Sorry," Monet said, lowering her head.

"Don't do that!" Hunter snapped.

"What?" Monet asked.

"Lower your head like that. It looks like you are defeated, and that's never going to happen. You need to be strong like your brother and show the NPCs of Minecraft that the sister of the User-that-is-not-a-user cannot be defeated by anything." Hunter placed a hand on her small zombie shoulders and looked down into her dark eyes. "Never give up on your friends and your family. And since you are here with Gameknight999, you are now part of our family. Now stand tall and remind everyone, NPCs and monsters alike, that Monet113 cannot be defeated, no matter how afraid you are inside."

Monet raised her head and looked up into Hunter's eyes, then smiled and stood a little taller.

"That's it," Hunter said, then turned to face the rest of the party. "Anyone remember where we left the horses?"

"We left them tied to that tree," Crafter said.

The young NPC moved to the tree and was shocked at what he saw . . . six sets of horse armor floating on the ground. Something had gotten the horses . . . probably spiders.

Hunter moved to Crafter's side and looked down at the ground.

"I guess we're on foot for now," she said. "Maybe we should start running."

"I agree," Woodcutter said. "But which way?"

"I have an idea, follow me," Gameknight said.

I hope you're watching, my friend, Gameknight thought. *We sure could use some help.*

Sprinting with all their speed, the group shot through the roofed forest, not slowing for stealth or to hide their path. They all knew that this was a race for their very lives, and speed was all that mattered. As they ran past a giant red mushroom, Gameknight looked over his shoulder expecting the zombie king to appear at any time between the thick trunks of the dark oaks. The look of surprise on the monster's face when he'd blocked his sword was something he'd always remember. Xa-Tul was terrifying, and the image of the hateful monster would likely haunt his dreams for a while.

Gameknight shuddered.

"Hey, you won't believe what I found," Hunter said as she reached the top of a small hill and started down the other side.

When Gameknight reached the crest two steps later, he was relieved by what he saw: a chest surrounded by torches. It looked like a bonus chest that can sometimes be found within Minecraft, but Gameknight knew better.

"What's in it?" he asked.

"Bread, cookies, some melon, and my favorite . . . arrows," Hunter said.

She scooped up the materials, then gave some arrows and food to Crafter and Woodcutter.

"Sorry, nothing here for zombies," Hunter said as she turned and continued to run. "I wonder how this came to be here?"

Gameknight smiled and said nothing.

Shawny, Gameknight thought, *Bring my sister back . . . use the digitizer with the settings reversed.*

There was a moment of silence, then a series of words flashed through his mind.

I can't, it's overheated, Shawny said. *I think it became too hot when we sent you into the game. Right now, the temperature indicator still puts it in the red. I can't bring her back right now.*

"Great," he said aloud.

"What now?" Hunter asked.

"The digitizer . . . I mean, the Gateway of Light won't work right now," Gameknight explained. "My sister is stuck in here with us for a while."

"Then she can enjoy this little run with us," she said as she continued to sprint.

They continued going for a few minutes, then came to a deep wide river, a narrow dirt bridge spanning the watery obstacle. On the other side of the river, they could see that the landscape changed from the roofed forest to a normal spruce forest. Gameknight felt a little better being able to see the sky. *At least we can see if there are any spiders up there above us,* he thought. Going single file, the group moved quickly across the river, but at the end of the bridge, Hunter could see a trip wire placed on the ground, an incomplete redstone circuit nearby.

"What's this all about?" she asked as she jumped past the wire.

Gameknight reached the end of the bridge and jumped off, careful to stay away from the trip wire. Turning around, he could see that if something hit the trip wire, it would cause the entire bridge to detonate.

It was a perfect trap.

Gameknight smiled again.

"OK, what's going on?" Crafter asked.

"It's my friend, Shawny," Gameknight explained. "He's watching us and entering Minecraft to set up these traps for us. He knows that he can't just appear because both of you will have to stop running and link your hands, so he's staying hidden."

Crafter looked at Hunter then back at Gameknight, a look of surprise on his boxy face.

"Yes, I told him all about the Convention of Crafters and the decision," Gameknight explained. "He knows that the users can't come and intervene without stopping all the NPCs from fighting. We are on our own . . . almost."

Suddenly, a loud guttural yell suddenly burst out of the forest. It was a sound that was filled with such overwhelming hatred and rage that it actually made everyone's ears hurt. But it wasn't just a scream . . . it was something different. Gameknight could feel it resonate within the fabric of Minecraft, calling out to all the creatures nearby.

"That sounded like Xa-Tul, the zombie king," Monet said.

"You named him?" Hunter said playfully. "They're always harder to get rid of after you give them a name." She then laughed as she pulled out an arrow and fitted it to her bow.

Instantly, they heard the clicking of spiders, and could see a large group of the black menaces moving through the forest, closing in on them like a deadly vise from both sides. There were at least eight of the creatures, their clicking getting louder as they moved in.

Crafter knelt down and finished setting the redstone trap, then everyone turned and continued their trek, squeezing every bit of speed they could out of their boxy legs.

"Crafter," Gameknight said, pointing as he ran.

"I see them," the young NPC replied as he fitted an arrow to his bow.

Turning, Gameknight looked down at his sister. He could see fear percolating within her dark eyes and knew that she was afraid. Drawing his own sword, he moved closer to her, running in lock step.

"Don't worry, we'll be alright," Gameknight said.

"You think I need a sword?" she asked.

"Have you ever used one in Minecraft before?"

"No," she said, her voice now cracking with fear.

"Then I think it's best if you just watch our backs and make sure that no monsters are sneaking up on us."

"You mean watch out for creepers?" she asked.

Gameknight nodded.

"Watch out for creepers," he affirmed, "amongst other things."

The spiders approached, the black fuzzy vise closing in on them. As the big monsters moved to cut off their path, likely an answer to Xa-Tul's call, Gameknight could tell that there was something different about these creatures. They looked angrier than in the past, their eyes filled with hatred and a hunger for violence. These spiders meant business, and he doubted that they would back down. It was time to fight, and with eight monsters standing before them, their odds were not good.

CHAPTER 23
THE SISTERS

The clicking sounds from the spiders filled the air, causing goose-bumps to form on Gameknight's green arms. They sounded enraged, ready for war, and hungry for a fight. Glancing at them, Gameknight shuddered.

Looking down at his sister, he felt a huge weight of responsibility for her safety. He hated always having to watch out for her, but that was his job when his father was away; he was the oldest.

But why did he have to always be gone?

Gameknight missed having his dad home, and hated all this responsibility. Looking back to his sister, he shivered at the thought of those spiders reaching her. He was still mad that she had pulled this stunt, but he was also filled with fear. He had to do something about those monsters, but he knew that they were only one of his problems; there was still a massive invasion of zombies on their tail.

No, I won't lose her now, not here, he thought. *I worked too hard to find her! I won't let her get hurt here, not while I still have breath in my lungs. It's my job to get her home safely and I refuse to fail!*

And then one of the puzzle pieces clicked in place. Gameknight came to a halt at the edge of a clearing, a forest of tall oaks ringing the area.

"Everyone get to cover and wait for me," Gameknight said. "When it's time, I'll need you all to come out fighting."

"How will we know when?" Crafter asked.

"Don't worry, you'll know."

At the center of the clearing, Gameknight could see the spiders coming together into a large group directly in front of them. The creatures scuttled about, nervously waiting to see what would happen. But then Gameknight moved toward the spiders, betting his life that they would not attack. They looked at the approaching zombie with curiosity, their clicking getting louder.

He counted eight of them, their red eyes glaring at the NPCs. Heading for the largest of the spiders, he moved quickly, his golden sword held out in front. As he neared he could hear whispers from the monsters, something that surprised him.

They were talking to each other . . . spiders . . . talking!

Ignoring the sounds, Gameknight moved directly in front of the largest monster. Its red eyes burned bright as its grey mandibles clicked together, its razor-sharp claws reflecting the rosy light of the setting sun.

Suddenly, there was a massive explosion off in the distance, the blast filling the night sky with light and sound. Gameknight smiled.

Thanks Shawny.

And then he leapt forward, swinging his golden sword with all his might. The attack caught the spider by complete surprise. Unable to understand what was happening, the spiders just stood there, shocked by what was happening. Swinging his blade again and again, he tore into the monster before him, knocking its HP down to zero before it knew what was going on. He then turned to the next spider and attacked as the giant arachnids started to finally move.

Suddenly, Monet stepped forward and yelled at the spiders, "Hey, over here, we're your friends. Hey, look at me."

The red eyes of the spiders all turned toward the young zombie, a look of confusion on their hideous faces. Using her most convincing zombie voice, Monet talked to the spiders, trying to distract them from the attacker that was tearing into their companions.

"Hey, I'm talking to you. What are you doing?"

The spiders were now completely confused. As they tried to figure out what was going on, Gameknight continued his attack until finally the spiders came to their senses and turned on him. At that moment, three arrows flew through the air and struck one of the spiders, Hunter's flaming arrow lighting the beast aflame. Its HP fell quickly until all that was left was a ball of silk thread and three balls of XP.

Gameknight sprinted, avoiding their terrible claws while striking out at them with his sword. Then Hunter stepped out into the open, as if daring them to attack, firing her enchanted bow with deadly accuracy. One of the spiders charged toward Monet, but Hunter's arrows quickly put it down. Crafter then moved out from behind a tree and stood next to Hunter. His bow sang a harmonious tune with Hunter's as his arrows found their targets. The spiders turned, ignoring Gameknight, and charged at Hunter and Crafter. But then Woodcutter stepped out from behind some bushes and added his fire from the side of the clearing, his arrows sinking into spider flesh.

The spiders tried to scatter, but the three enticing targets standing out in the open was too much to resist. Charging toward their enemies, the spiders scuttled straight at them, ignoring the deranged zombie at their backs . . . that was a mistake. As the spider ran, Gameknight sliced away at them, tearing into backs and slashing at legs. With quick, well-timed attacks, he destroyed one spider, then another and another as they closed the distance. While this was happening,

Crafter and Hunter were concentrating their attacks on the same spider, combining the lethal power of their arrows. Another spider popped and disappeared as its HP was consumed, then another, and another. Lacking any leadership or battle plan, the spiders just fought for themselves instead of working together; they were no match for the combined arrows and Gameknight's blade. By the time the spiders reached the NPC's position, there was only one left.

Now, with victory turned to defeat in a blink of an eye, the remaining spider no longer clicked its mandibles so loudly. Moving back a few steps, the creature bumped into Gameknight999. Turning, it glared up at the zombie with hateful eyes.

"Why doesss a green help the NPCssss?" the spider said, its hissing voice reminding Gameknight of some kind of snake.

Looking down on the creature, the User-that-is-not-a-user said nothing, just held his golden sword tight. Then Monet moved to her brother's side.

"We don't have to kill this spider do we?" she asked. "There's been enough violence."

"The green child talkssss like an NPC . . . I now undersssstand," the spider said. Half of its burning red eyes glanced at Hunter and Crafter while the other half turned and looked at Woodcutter who was still standing near the edge of the clearing. "The sistersss will stop the NPCsss and help the greensss take over," the spider said proudly. "The Maker has called Shaikulud to hisssss side. We will be there when the NPCssss are destroyed."

"What are you talking about?" Gameknight asked.

"Just kill it and be done with it," Hunter snapped as she drew back her arrow and aimed at the creature's head.

Just then, the sound of zombie moans filled the

air from all sides . . . they were trying to surround Gameknight and his friends. As the User-that-is-not-a-user turned toward the noise, the spider jumped at him, its wicked curved claws reaching out for his zombie flesh. But it never had a chance. Hunter, Crafter, and Woodcutter all fired at the same time, hitting the monster with arrows while it was in mid air. It disappeared with a pop before Gameknight even turned back around.

The moans sounded again, this time a little closer.

"I think it best that we get moving," Crafter said.

"You think?" Hunter added as she notched another arrow to her bow.

Suddenly, Woodcutter screamed as a small cave spider leapt out of the shadows and attacked, biting at the NPC with its poisonous fangs. He moved backward, swinging his bow at the creature, trying to keep it away. It did little good. The dark blue monster leapt forward. Its fangs sank into Woodcutter's leg, causing him to scream and fall backward. It then tried to jump on top of him, but he was able to get an arrow fitted to his bow. Firing when it was nearly on top of him, his arrow sank into its soft belly. The cave spider screamed out in pain and moved back a step. Woodcutter struggled to his feet as he fitted another arrow to his bowstring, but the damage had already been done

Just then, a flaming arrow streaked through the air and hit the cave spider in the side. It flashed red. Then another arrow from Crafter's bow added to the fray. Sprinting forward, Gameknight moved to Woodcutter's side, his golden sword slashing down on the monster, landing lethal hits again and again. With multiple arrows sticking out of its dark blue fuzzy body, its HP finally was consumed and it disappeared, a look of ferocious hatred in its multiple eyes.

"That was close," Monet said as she moved to her

brother's side.

But then Woodcutter dropped his bow and fell to the ground, a sickly look to his skin. Small green swirls of light seemed to emanate from his body as if he were giving off some kind of toxic gas. Ignoring the particle effect, Gameknight rushed to his side and held the dying NPC in his arms.

"I'm glad I had the chance to fight at the side of the User-that-is-not-a-user one more time," Woodcutter said, then gave off a painful cough. "Who would have thought I'd need milk out here in a forest."

"Milk?" Monet asked.

"Milk is the only antidote to the cave spider's poison," Crafter explained. "If someone is only bitten once, then they may survive, but if bitten many times then milk is the only chance of survival against the terrible poison."

"Then someone give him some milk," Monet exclaimed.

"We don't have any, kid," Hunter replied.

"You mean he's going to . . . "

Hunter nodded.

Monet looked down at Woodcutter, and a small square tear flowed down her cheek.

"We have to do something for him," she said as she knelt down at his side.

"There's nothing that can be done, sister to the User-that-is-not-a-user," Woodcutter said. "Sometimes . . . "

Suddenly a zombie growl echoed through the forest; the monster horde was getting closer.

"You must leave," Woodcutter said, his voice filled with sadness . . . and a final burst of strength. "I cannot go with you, my friends. You must leave me behind."

"No, we can't do that," Monet said as she looked

up into Crafter's blue eyes.

"You have no choice," Woodcutter added as he picked up his bow and notched an arrow. "I will delay them as long as I can."

"No . . . " Monet said, but Hunter grabbed her by the arm and pulled her away, running away from the monster sounds.

"Come on!" Hunter shouted as she ran.

Crafter looked down at Woodcutter, then gave him a nod, then stepped back and scanned their surroundings, looking for threats. Gameknight, still holding him in his zombie arms, propped him up and positioned him so that he back was against a tall pine tree.

"You have to stop this zombie invasion and save our people . . . " Woodcutter said hoarsely, then coughed violently. "My family . . . you have to keep them safe."

"I will do what I can," Gameknight replied, then patted him on the shoulder, his dark claws standing out against his red smock. "You will be remembered."

Woodcutter grunted.

"GO!"

Gameknight gave him a sad nod, then turned and sprinted after his friends, knowing full well what was about to happen to that NPC. But would the rest of them escape Woodcutter's fate?

Shuddering, Gameknight sprinted with all the speed he could muster to catch up with Hunter and his sister, Crafter at his side.

"I HATE THIS!" Gameknight yelled. "The Woodcutter twins are now gone . . . and for what?"

"For your sister," Crafter replied. "The sister of the User-that-is-not-a-user is important to all NPCs. You saved us all, and now they are giving back . . . the only way they know how."

Sprinting in silence, they could see Hunter and Monet113 ahead; they were slowly closing in on them.

"Why does he have to be gone so much?!" Gameknight said, his voice filled with anger as he thought about his dad. "Why do I have to be the responsible one . . . he should be here so that I can be just a kid! I hate being responsible for my little sister . . . she does the dumbest things."

"Perhaps . . . but she is your sister . . . your family, and family is a precious thing. The special thing about family is that they'll always be there for you, sometimes when you least expect it. You never know when you're going to need help, and you can always count on your family." Crafter paused and pulled back an arrow as he heard a sound from the woods. As they ran, he saw it was just a cow walking through the forest, crunching some dead twigs with its hooves. Releasing his draw, he moved closer to Gameknight999 so that his words would be clearly heard. "Family is a wonderful thing, even when they are aggravating and make you crazy. But there is a special bond between brothers and sisters that can never be replaced. Cherish it for as long as you can."

Gameknight nodded and considered his young friend's wise words as he ran, the sounds of the angry zombie army close on their heels.

CHAPTER 24

THE VILLAGE

As Gameknight caught up to his friends, the sounds of zombies grew louder, their angry growls and sorrowful moans filling the air. The monster horde had caught up to them while they had been battling the spiders, and now they were close behind . . . too close.

"I hope Woodcutter is going to be alright," Monet said nervously.

"He is a good NPC, but he knew the risk when he agreed to come with us," Hunter said. "He knows where his responsibility lies."

Suddenly, a loud scream pierced through the forest. It was the sound of surprise and pain from a zombie. And then there was another scream . . . and another . . . and another.

Hunter looked at Monet and smiled.

"Woodcutter is making them pay dearly," Hunter said, a ring of pride in her voice.

"But the zombies don't seem to be slowing much," Crafter added.

Gameknight listened and could still hear the sounds of pursuit as they ran, the shuffling of clumsy zombie feet crunching through the bushes and their animal-like growls filling the air. He wished it didn't have to come to this. Unlike Hunter, the sound of any living thing in pain brought a sadness to his heart.

"We have to go faster," Hunter said as she ran.

"Maybe I should leave a few more surprises,"

Crafter suggested.

"No, just run," the User-that-is-not-a-user said as he glanced nervously over his shoulder.

As they threaded their way through the forest, Gameknight999 thought about the impending battle. Based on the monsters he saw coming out of those deep tunnels in zombie-town, he figured there must be hundreds of monsters pursuing them, maybe even a thousand. It was as if all the zombies from the other servers had been brought here to chase him. He shuddered as he pictured the violence about to descend upon this server. What if he couldn't find a solution to this problem? What if he wasn't strong enough or smart enough to protect his sister and his friends? What if . . . every possible disaster played through his head like a terrible movie, driving his courage into the darkest recesses of his soul.

No, I won't be afraid of what might *happen,* he thought. *I'm focusing on the* now *and not the* what if.

Gameknight drove the images from his mind. Instead, he thought about all the puzzle pieces before him . . . the massive zombie army . . . Xa-Tul, the zombie king . . . his sister . . . He considered everything that was happening and looked for a solution that would save his friends, and hopefully himself as well.

But he came up with nothing.

And as worry started to creep back into his mind, he heard Hunter cheering ahead of him. In the distance, between the tall pine trees and low hanging branches, Gameknight could see light, a grassy plain with torches planted in the ground. And beyond the plain were the tall, fortified walls of Crafter's village.

"We made it!" Monet113 exclaimed.

As they ran from the edge of the forest, Gameknight saw two-block high structures everywhere before them. Beneath each was a 3x3 hole filled with water:

Romantist's arrow bombs! The blocks that were stacked above the water looked almost fuzzy, as if a million porcupines sat on each. But as they neared, Gameknight could tell that they were not spines, but arrows stuck in the blocks, hundreds impaled in each stack, and there were countless stacks spread out all across the plain.

Gameknight smiled. Digger had been busy while they had been gone.

An angry, howling growl came from the forest behind them. It echoed across the landscape and was probably heard for miles.

"Quickly, run for the gates," Crafter said as he looked at Gameknight, fear in his blue eyes starting to change to panic. "It's our only chance."

But just as the howling echo started to fade, a huge collection of monsters emerged ahead of them from the left side of the forest. The green wave of creatures flowed across the grassy plain, trampling on flowers and crushing bushes as they moved across their path, cutting off their escape. The creatures stopped just out of bow range from the village and turned toward the NPCs. Snarling at their soon-to-be victims, the zombies moaned and growled excitedly.

Then the forest behind them exploded with zombie bodies as those pursuing them finally emerged from the foliage, Xa-Tul at the head of the column, his massive form towering over the rest of his subjects.

They were trapped.

Gameknight stopped running and grabbed his sister's arm, pulling her to his side. He then drew his golden sword as he surveyed the situation. They were completely surrounded and had no hope of surviving the attack that was sure to come. There were probably five hundred zombies coming out of the forest, and another couple hundred standing before them, cutting off their escape. Even with the fortifications of Crafter's village and all the redstone traps within the walls, the NPCs within the village also stood no chance of survival. They may be able to make a good accounting of themselves and make the zombies pay dearly, but surely every villager in the city would die.

Looking back at the fortified wall, Gameknight could see the broad-shouldered form of Digger standing tall on the wall, his pointed pickaxe held over his shoulder (a terrifyingly lethal weapon in his hands). An image of Digger's children, Topper and Filler, popped into Gamekight's head.

Would they have to die as well?

He then looked down at his sister as fear slithered down his spine.

No . . . it can't end like this.

Suddenly, something happened deep in the forest. A popping sound echoed across the battlefield as something materialized between the pine trees. In the distance, Gameknight could see a narrow thread of light appear, the glowing beam stretching up high into the air.

A server thread . . . it was Shawny!

An arrow then flew from the forest and arced through the air. The zombies all watched its path as it flew high overhead, curving gracefully through the air until it came down into one of the zombies that stood between the NPCs and the safety of the fortified walls.

"One arrow," Xa-Tul boomed. "Is that what confronts this zombie army?"

The zombie king then gave off a loud maniacal laugh that slowly percolated throughout the entire monster army, all of the zombies snickering a growling sort of sound that made the tiny hairs on Gameknight's arms stand up.

But then suddenly, a hundred threads of light appeared within the forest . . . then a hundred more off to the right . . . and another hundred to the left. As if on command, three hundred arrows erupted from the forest and flew through the air, darkening the light from the moon as they flew through the air. Before they landed, another volley leapt up into the air.

Confused, the zombies stood and watched the deadly projectiles curve overhead. And as the cloud of arrows landed amidst the zombie army, howls of pain and surprise filled the air. Just before the second volley landed, a single voice range out from the forest. Gameknight recognized the voice instantly.

"RUN!" Shawny voice sounded from deep in the forest.

Grabbing Monet's hand, Gameknight sprinted straight toward the group of zombies that stood between them and the village gates. Many zombies had been killed in the first wave of arrows, but the remaining zombies were getting ready for Gameknight's charge. Either they were too dumb or too distracted to notice the second volley of arrows. The pointed barbs fell down on the monsters like a lethal rain, erasing the remaining monsters from the face of Minecraft and opening a pathway to the village.

Xa-Tul screamed out in frustration, then punched the nearest zombie, reducing its HP to half with the single blow.

"WHAT IS THIS TREACHERY?" he bellowed. "STOP THEM!"

Sprinting with all their speed, Gameknight, Monet, Hunter, and Crafter all ran for the safety of the village . . . but the zombies were now moving as well. The group of green monsters off to the left was too close. Moving quicker than he'd ever seen zombies move, the monsters sprinted forward. They were going to cut off their escape. Would they make it in time?

Glancing at the approaching zombies, Gameknight could see that the monsters would make it to the gates before them . . . they were lost.

Suddenly, the ground erupted with thunder as fifty horses burst from the gates and charged straight into the approaching army. To his surprise, he saw the armor-clad figure of Stitcher leading the charge, her flowing red hair streaming behind her as if she were on fire. Riding with all their speed they charged straight for the oncoming monster horde.

"FOR MINECRAFT!" the cavalry yelled as they road toward their attackers.

The sound brought forth a cheer from the fortified walls as archers on the battlements started to open fire on the advancing zombies. The cavalry smashed into the approaching zombie army and tore into them with the ferocity of an unstoppable storm. Iron swords rang out as they smashed down into zombie flesh, rending HP from rotting bodies. The front wave of the monster charge fell in seconds as the cavalry spun around and readied a second charge. The surviving monsters, seeing all of their comrades converted to glowing balls of XP, stopped their charge. This gave Gameknight and his friends the time to make it to the gates.

"Stitcher, come back inside!" Gameknight yelled as he ushered his sister through the gates, Crafter and Hunter right on her heels.

Glancing to the gates, Stitcher gave the command and the cavalry wheeled around and headed for the village gates. The zombies, realizing that the cavalry charge was no longer a threat, continued their advance on the village, but the rain of arrows that fell down upon them from the tall dirt walls caused them to rethink this attack. Running away from the village, the zombies moved out of arrow range and stopped. They milled about, growling and moaning as they glared up at the defenders on the battlements.

Waiting for the cavalry to all get into the village, Gameknight stood next to the gate, his golden sword in his hand. The mounted warriors drew their swords as they approached the gates, unsure of this armed zombie, but then Crafter stepped out and stood next to Gameknight, waving the soldiers back into the village. As they rode by, they gave Gameknight suspicious looks, but the presence of their crafter eased their fears a bit.

"Well done, Stitcher," Gameknight said as she finally rode through the gates, a look of confusion on her face.

With everyone safely inside the village, Gameknight and Crafter stepped inside, pulling the iron doors closed. But as the User-that-is-not-a-user turned around, he found a hundred arrows pointed at his head, his sister surrounded by swordsmen.

"What are you all doing," Crafter shouted. "This is Gameknight999 and his sister. Put your weapons down right now!"

Many of them lowered their weapons, but the presence of a zombie within the village walls was too terrifying.

"You heard him you idiots," Hunter snapped. "These are friends, not enemies, now put down your weapons or you'll have to answer to me!"

Moving next to Monet, she put her arm around the young zombie and hugged her tight.

"Who would have thought I'd ever be doing this," she whispered to Monet113.

The young zombie smiled.

The warriors lowered their weapons as Crafter stepped forward with Gameknight999 at his side.

"Friends, this is the User-that-is-not-a-user and

his sister, both in zombie disguises," Crafter said to the crowd. "Rest assured, they are not zombies. They are our friends and they are here to help us."

"But what about that zombie army out there?" someone yelled from the crowd of villagers. "How can he help us against that?"

"The User-that-is-not-a-user was able to help save Minecraft once before," Crafter explained. "He is here again at our time of need."

Some of the villagers cheered, but most just looked uncertain and afraid. They had all seen the massive zombie army at their doorstep, and they all knew that their defenses could not stop an attack of that size.

"What do we do, Gameknight999?" another asked from the crowd.

Gameknight stepped forward and looked at the scared boxy faces and knew that he had to help them. But then, a clawed hand found his own and its fingers intertwined between his own. Looking down, he saw his sister standing next to him, holding his hand, a scared look on her face.

"First things first," he muttered.

Closing his eyes, he reached out with his mind, feeling for the mechanism that drove Minecraft. Imagining himself at his keyboard, he mentally pushed the letters, sending out a message to his friend.

Shawny, try the digitizer again. Aim it at my sister and reverse the settings . . . do it NOW.

Releasing his sister's hand, he took a step away from her. Confused, she looked up at his brother.

"What is it?" she asked, but Gameknight remained silent.

He stood there, looking down on his sister . . . but nothing happened.

Shawny, what's happening . . . use the digitizer and bring her back . . . now!

Nothing . . . only silence.

But then a nervous voice crept into his head.

It's not working, Gameknight, Shawny said. *I think some component got fried. I can smell smoke coming from the electronics somewhere. I'm looking through the components. If I can find it, I can take something from one of the other inventions down here in the basement. But for right now, it's not working . . . sorry . . . it's dead.*

Then so are we, Gameknight thought.

"It's not working," he said to his sister as he stepped forward. "The digitizer is broken and can't be used to get you back right now."

"What?!"

"It's OK," he lied, "Shawny is working on it. He'll find out what's wrong and get it fixed as soon as he can. In the mean time, we just need to stay away from monsters and keep out of danger."

Hunter laughed. "Easier said than done . . . especially right now."

Behind the village walls, they could hear the massive zombie army gathering, their sorrowful moans and angry growls filling the air like an approaching, unavoidable storm.

"Tommy . . . I'm scared," Monet whispered to her brother.

"I know . . . me too," he replied as he put his zombie arm around her shoulder. "But don't worry. I won't let anything happen to you . . . I never will."

Looking up at her brother, Monet smiled and rested her head on his gold-coated chest.

But then, Gameknight's blood turned to ice as he heard Xa-Tul's voice echo across the landscape.

"GET READY TO ATTACK!" the zombie king growled. "LEAVE NONE ALIVE."

The villagers screamed in terror. Many grabbed

their children's hands and ran back to their homes, hoping their wooden door would stop the hundreds and hundreds of zombies that stood outside their fortified walls.

Gameknight knew better.

I have to do something to help these people . . . my friends . . . my sister. But what?

The pieces of the puzzle started to tumble around in his head. There was a solution here, something that would save all these lives, but what was it? Xa-Tul's voice had triggered a memory . . . a zombie memory and knowledge about how zombie clans were ruled. The zombie mod must have worked so well that Gameknight had access to all the knowledge that real zombies took for granted . . . *Only the strongest can lead,* the memory said.

One of the puzzle pieces fell into place.

Taking a step toward the village gates, another of the pieces found its home, the solution slowly taking form in his mind. Taking another step forward, more pieces of the puzzle found their place.

"Gameknight, what are you doing?" Hunter asked.

Reaching out, he grasped his sister's hand, then put it into Hunter's blocky grip.

"I need you to take care of her, Hunter," Gameknight said, a deadly serious tone to his voice. "I'm relying on you."

Hunter put aside her sarcastic remarks and answered him, friend to friend.

"I will protect her with my life," she replied.

"What's happening?" Monet asked, clearly confused.

"What are you doing?" Crafter asked. "What's going on?"

Reaching out, he pushed on the lever that opened the iron doors. More pieces fell into place.

"What are you doing?" Monet asked . . . pleaded.

Ignoring his friends and sister, he stepped outside. And as the iron door slammed shut behind him, the last pieces of the puzzle fell into place. The sound of five hundred zombie growls filled his ears as he faced this monstrous threat alone. And amidst their howls of anger and hatred, Gameknight999 knew what he had to do.

CHAPTER 25

GAMEKNIGHT VS. XA-TUL

Gameknight walked away from the iron doors and headed straight toward Xa-Tul, the zombie king.

"Gameknight, what are you doing?" Crafter yelled.

Glancing over his shoulder, he could see his young friend now standing on the top of the wall, Hunter and Monet at his side.

"I'm doing what must be done," Gameknight replied.

"You're being an idiot," Hunter shouted. "Get back in here . . . please . . . "

Smiling at her, he turned and continued to walk toward Xa-Tul. Staring straight ahead, he could see the almost continuous wall of green bodies, their light blue shirts reminding him of the color of the sky at noon . . . funny he'd never noticed that before. In the distance, he could see that the mass of server threads from the forest were all gone . . . the users had left. Off to the right, he could see splashes of color amidst the monsters, bright stripes of red and yellow and white and pink: the zombie children that Monet had befriended, but it was more than before. Gameknight smiled. Apparently Monet had infected them with an idea . . . and it was contagious. These colorful zombies did not look as menacing as the others. In fact, there was something completely different about them. They seemed to stand a little taller, more confident for some reason, but not more violent. It was as if they were seeing this situation through a different perspective than the other zombies . . . all because of a few spots of color.

"Leave it to you lil' sis' to stir things up, even in Zombie-town," Gameknight said to himself.

As he moved across the battlefield, he could hear the zombies closing in behind, completely surrounding him. When he reached the stacked blocks of TNT, he stopped and glared at Xa-Tul. Drawing his golden sword, he pointed at the zombie king.

"I CHALLENGE XA-TUL FOR LEADERSHIP OF THE CLAN!"

A nervous calm spread across the zombie army as all growls and moans ceased. It was quiet as a coffin; Gameknight could hear the rustle of the leaves on the trees and the swishing of the blades of grass as a cool breeze blew across the plain. The music of Minecraft played subtly within those sounds, filling his ears with beauty.

It's funny how you notice these little things just as you are about to face your own death, he thought.

A booming laugh came from the zombie king.

"This is not a challenge to Xa-Tul, it is a joke," the zombie king yelled. "The death of this challenger will be a lesson to all."

Gameknight then drew a line in the ground with his golden sword.

"This is as far as you go, Xa-Tul," Gameknight yelled back. "I'm stopping you right here!"

Xa-Tul laughed again, then started to walk toward him, the toothy smile on his face turning to a snarl. Gameknight could hear the clinking of his chain mail as he crossed the field. It almost sounded like wind chimes . . . very deadly wind chimes.

I hope you're there, Shawny, Gameknight thought, pressing the keys of his keyboard in his mind. *I think I'm going to need you really soon!*

He waited for a response, but received none . . . only silence.

Shawny, where are you . . . are you there . . . I really need you right now . . . Shawny . . . Shawny . . .

And then his voice filled his head.

Sorry, I'm here now, Shawny said. *But you should . . .*

Nevermind about that, are you watching what's going on? Gameknight said.

Sure, but I need to tell you that . . .

Later, I just need you to be ready with the digitizer, get it fixed . . . fast. I'll let you know when I'm ready, but for now, don't talk or distract me. I have the zombie king coming at me and I need to concentrate.

But . . .

NOT NOW!

OK . . .

"So, this pathetic zombie challenges for leadership of the clan," Xa-Tul said as he approached.

"I'm not challenging for leadership of the clan, I'm taking it!" Gameknight responded.

Xa-Tul smiled, then drew his massive golden sword. He could hear the zombies moving closer to watch this historic battle.

Good, that's where I want all you zombies, close to me, Gameknight thought. *That's right, come closer . . . all of you.*

"What is the name of this foolish zombie that challenges Xa-Tul?" the zombie king asked.

"You aren't worthy of knowing my name," Gameknight replied. "And besides, it won't matter when I destroy you."

"Very well, if the name will not be given, then Xa-Tul will call this zombie Fool," the zombie king replied. "Is Fool ready to do battle with Xa-Tul?"

As his answer, Gameknight charged forward, swinging his golden sword at the zombie king. The speed and ferocity of the attack clearly surprised Xa-Tul, for he missed his first slash, Gameknight's blade digging into the monster's chain mail. Howling in frustration, Xa-Tul battled back, swinging his massive blade at Gameknight's head. Ducking under the attack, he stabbed at the zombie's legs, hoping to pierce a thigh, but his sword was deflected by the chainmail that hung at the monster's waist.

SMASH!

Xa-Tul's blade crashed into Gameknight's side, cracking his chest plate. Pain radiated throughout his body as he struggled for breath. He hadn't even seen that attack coming. The strength of this creature was amazing. If he hadn't been wearing this golden armor, he would likely have been killed. Reaching down, he could feel the crack that now ran along his side, the sword doing significant damage to his armor.

The zombie king laughed, then brought his sword down on Gameknight again. This time, though, he was ready and brought up his own sword in time to block the blow.

CRASH!

The swords smashed together. The shock of the blow moved down his arms, almost knocking the sword from his hands, the blade getting cracked and chipped. He had to move faster, only blocking his blows would end in defeat. Then one of the quotes from Sun Tzu that were stuck up on his teacher's wall came to mind: "Be where your enemy is not." That's it . . . Gameknight had to be where Xa-Tul didn't expect him, but this zombie body was just too slow.

Swinging his sword at the monster's side, Gameknight landed a glancing blow on the monster's armor, but it did little damage. Spinning, he tried to slash at the zombie's arm, but blade met blade and bounced harmlessly away.

BOOM!

Xa-Tul landed another blow to Gameknight, this time splitting his armor in half, causing it to fall off his body. The blow completely knocked the wind out of him, forcing him to his knees. If Xa-Tul landed another hit . . . he was dead.

Shawny . . . now . . . bring me back.

I can't, he answered. *I haven't found the dead component yet. It's still not working. I can't do anything.*

Oh no . . . I'm stuck here, again, and Xa-Tul is about to finish me off, Gameknight thought to himself.

The puzzle pieces rearranged in his head.

"Behold, the Fool . . . the newest challenger is about to be destroyed," Xa-Tul boomed, his burning, hateful eyes scanning his zombie army to make sure that all were watching. "None can challenge Xa-Tul and survive."

Suddenly, Gameknight knew what to do.

Shawny, turn off the zombie mod on my computer . . . quick.

Will it affect you and your sister? Shawny asked.

No, I'm running a second application of Minecraft on the digitizer's computer, just turn off the zombie mod on my Minecraft session . . . do it QUICK!

Instantly, a burning green glow came from

Gameknight999, making Xa-Tul step back a pace or two. The ball of light grew bigger and bigger until it completely enveloped Gameknight's zombie body, making all the monsters on the field of battle shield their eyes. Uncertain what was happening, Xa-Tul took another step backward and growled.

"What magic is this?" the zombie king complained. "Quit these games and face me, Fool."

And as the bright green glow dissipated, Xa-Tul found himself facing a user clad in diamond armor, an enchanted diamond sword in his hand.

Standing, Gameknight faced the monster, the letters in his name glowing brightly above his head. Reaching into his inventory, he pulled out a potion of healing and drank it quickly, then threw the bottle to the ground at the zombie king's feet.

"My name isn't Fool, it's Gameknight999, the User-that-is-not-a-user," he said loudly.

The NPCs on the village wall all cheered and waved their weapons high overhead. Not taking his eyes off his adversary, he raised his sword up high and waved it to his friends, then lowered it and readied it for the next attack.

"I'm tired of *your* foolishness," Gameknight snapped. "Come on zombie . . . let's dance!"

CHAPTER 26

GAMEKNIGHT999'S BATTLE

Standing, Gameknight999 glared at the gigantic zombie before him. Xa-Tul had a look of complete surprise on his hideous face, his dark eyes burning red with hatred.

"Now you face the real me," Gameknight said. "And I think you will find that I am not as slow as I was in that zombie body."

"The Fool talks too much," Xa-Tul growled.

Swinging his massive golden sword, the zombie king advanced, trying to strike at Gameknight's head. Rolling to the side, the blade easily missed him. As he stood, Gameknight slashed at the zombie king's legs, cracking the chain mail and causing huge pieces to fall off. Sprinting behind his enemy, Gameknight swung his enchanted blade at the creature's back, however the monster anticipated this and stepped away, just out of range.

Turning, Xa-Tul charged straight at Gameknight, his sword swinging wildly. Moving to the side, his diamond sword struck at the creature again. The shimmering blade tore more of the chain mail from the huge green muscular chest. The zombie king howled in frustration as he turned and charged again. But Gameknight was too fast. He jumped out of the way at the last instant. Turning, he brought his diamond sword down on the creature's shoulder.

Stopping to look at his adversary, Xa-Tul growled as he readied his next charge, but for the first time, Gameknight could see glimpses of fear in his blazing red eyes.

"Xa-Tul will destroy the Fool," the zombie bellowed.

"Now it's *you* that talks too much."

The zombie king growled, then stepped forward, swinging his sword with all his might. Knowing that he couldn't block those massive blows, Gameknight dropped to the ground and allowed the blade to streak over his head as he stabbed at the creature's stomach, his enchanted blade finding flesh.

The zombie flashed red.

Rolling across the ground just as the blade came crashing into the grass, Gameknight stood and slashed at the monster's arm with all his strength.

Flash . . . red . . . he'd scored another hit.

Xa-Tul screamed out in anger and pain, but before he could swing his sword again, Gameknight swung his blade at an exposed leg, then his chest, then his other arm.

Flash . . . red . . . red . . . red.

The monster fell to one knee for a moment, then stood up and readied another charge, but this time Gameknight was prepared. As the monster ran at him, the User-that-is-not-a-user stepped sideways and ducked. Swinging his sword at the monster while he streaked by, Gameknight scored hits on both legs.

Flash . . . red . . . red.

Xa-Tul fell to the ground with a thud. As he struggled to get up, Gameknight attacked. Slashing at his mailed back, he tore into the remnants of the creature's chain mail, the clinking armor falling to the ground. Once all of the creature's armor was gone, Gameknight999 stepped back and let the creature stand.

"It doesn't have to be like this," Gameknight said. "This does not have to be a battle to the death. NPCs and zombies do not have to be enemies."

Xa-Tul slowly climbed to his feet. Gameknight could see that he was in a lot of pain; his HP was dangerously low and they both knew it. But as he turned and glared at the User-that-is-not-a-user a vicious and evil smile slowly crept across his face.

"Xa-Tul was crafted for only one reason . . . to destroy the NPCs, and that is what must be done. Look around, Fool, the destruction of the NPCs is certain. This zombie army will be like an unstoppable storm as it sweeps across this server, grinding the villages into dust, and nothing short of a miracle can save these NPCs from extermination."

The monster then howled a zombie battle cry that was filled with such hatred and malice that it made Gameknight take a step back. In that instant, Xa-Tul charged, swinging his massive blade at Gameknight999's head. Dodging the attack, the User-that-is-not-a-user swung his own blade at the exposed stomach, striking deep, making the creature flash red. He then attacked at his side and back, swinging his enchanted sword with all his might, scoring hit after hit after hit.

Xa-Tul fell to the ground, his HP nearly depleted. Without the strength to stand, the zombie king just lay there, awaiting his fate. But before Gameknight999 could finish off the monster, a bright ball of white light formed next to the fallen zombie. The light grew brighter and spread across the grassy blocks. Looking down, Gameknight could see the blades of grass that touched the sphere of light turn grey, then brown, then black as if they were burnt . . . no, not burnt, but poisoned by some hateful disease. And as the foul stench of these dying blocks reached his nose, the light began to fade. Looking up, Gameknight found the bright-eyed shadow-crafter that he'd seen on the hilltop near the Source: the creature that had escaped into one of the server beacons. His dark and sinister form surprised the User-that-is-not-a-user and made him take a step back, unsure what to do.

Reaching down, the shadow-crafter placed a hand on Xa-Tul's shoulder, then teleported away, taking with him the wounded zombie king. And then in seconds, the shadow-crafter reappeared standing before Gameknight, a dark, shadowy sword in his hand.

"I have been looking for you, User-that-is-not-a-user, across all the server planes in the Minecraft universe," the creature said. "And now you stand before me."

The creature was clad in all black, its armor made of something Gameknight hadn't seen before in Minecraft, but it was something that looked familiar . . . somehow. The armor was dark, almost pitch black but with the faintest hint of deep purple to it. And then Gameknight realized what it was; the armor was giving off the tiniest of particles, small purple specks that hovered just around the surface, moving away then getting pulled back into the shadowy depths by some unseen currents. It reminded him of . . . no . . . it couldn't be.

"I've seen you before. You're one of those shadow-crafters, the creatures that are causing all this trouble within Minecraft," Gameknight said with a sneer.

"You are mistaken. I am not one of the shadow-crafters . . . I am *the* shadow-crafter, the Maker of all the others. I am Herobrine," he said maliciously, an eerie, sinister smile on his face. "I created Erebus and Malacoda just like I created my zombie king, Xa-Tul. My past creations failed to destroy Minecraft for me, but Xa-Tul did his task well."

Herobrine is real?! Gameknight thought, a shot of fear rippling through his body. *How could this be possible?* "And what was his task?" he asked, not sure if he really wanted to hear the answer.

"Why, he brought you before me . . . that was his task." Herobrine took a step forward and his white eyes grew bright, their ominous glow stretching to the edge of his square face. Nervously, Gameknight took a step back. "Now you will face *me* in battle and be destroyed."

"But why?" Gameknight asked. "Why must we battle?"

Herobrine laughed a maniacal laugh as if he knew some great secret.

"You will know . . . at the end," the evil shadow-crafter said. Turning, he gazed at the zombie army that watched. "All of you back up and do not interfere . . . give us room."

The zombies moved backward, creating a wide clearing.

Suddenly, Herobrine leapt forward, swinging his ominous dark sword. Gameknight brought his own enchanted blade up and blocked the attack. Their weapons clashed together, and in that moment when they met, Gameknight could see the small sparkling purple particles even closer. They danced around the surface as they moved on unseen currents, floating away from the weapon, then drawing back in. His eyes widened as he recognized them: the teleportation particles of an enderman.

"I see you recognize my creation," Herobrine said has he pulled his sword back. "This is the first of its kind: endersword and enderarmor, stronger than any metal your puny NPCs could craft and absolutely impenetrable."

Herobrine attacked again, this time feigning to the right then striking to the left. Gameknight saw the trick and ignored the former and blocked the latter, then charged forward, thrusting his diamond blade at Herobrine's exposed chest. The tip of his sword just passed through his black armor as if it were shadow, finding nothing underneath.

Herobrine laughed.

Gameknight stepped back and looked at the tip of his sword, seeing if it had been damaged, but it still had its razor-sharp appearance.

"Now you begin to understand," Herobrine laughed.

Jumping high in the air, the shadow-crafter swung his dark blade down at Gameknight. Rolling to his side, the User-that-is-not-a-user just narrowly avoided the attack, the shadowy sword clipping his side. Pain radiated through his body as if the blade were made of fire. He could feel cracks in his diamond armor, chunks of his protective coating falling to the ground.

Herobrine laughed.

As he stood, Gameknight charged forward, faking an attack to his head as he swung his diamond blade with all his might at his adversary's chest. Herobrine moved his endersword up to block the feint, but as he waved his dark blade at nothing, Gameknight swung the diamond sword into his enemy's chest. But again it met no resistance . . . no clash of sword with armor . . . no razor-sharp blade piercing flesh. His blade only felt air as it passed through Herobrine, a cloud of purple particles filling the air.

The shadow-crafter laughed again.

Stepping back, Gameknight stared at his opponent, the puzzle pieces starting to tumble within his head.

"Ahhh . . . he begins to understand," Herobrine mocked. "Yes, that's right, my enderarmor possesses the teleportation powers of the enderman that gave their life so that I could be so wonderfully clothed." Herobrine's eyes grew bright as he glared at Gameknight999. "When you attack, your blade is just teleported to somewhere else before it can reach my flesh, and when you pull it back, it teleports back. I am invulnerable to anything you can throw against me." Herobrine took a step closer to Gameknight, his eyes narrowing. "Your only chance is to run away, loser. Quick, take your pathetic Gateway of Light and escape before I kill you."

Gameknight stepped back. Herobrine was every bit as terrifying that the legends made him out to be. How would he defeat him?

I can't take the Gateway of Light, the digitizer is broken, he thought. *I have to figure this out.*

Looking across the battlefield, he could see that the zombies had started to move closer, the desire to see their leader vanquish Gameknight999 too great. He could see some of them moving around the stacked blocks of TNT, some of the zombies splashing through the water that surrounded the striped blocks.

And one of the pieces of the puzzle clicked into place.

As Herobrine gave him an eerie, sinister smile, Gameknight leapt forward, swinging his sword with all his strength. He attacked with a quick series of strikes, slashing at his enemy's head, then arm, then legs, each time causing Herobrine to block it with his sword and take a step back. Gameknight repeated the series . . . head . . . arms . . . legs, and again Herobrine blocked the attack. Gameknight did the same thing, but this time . . . head . . . legs . . . arms. Herobrine was not ready for the change, and Gameknight's blade slipped under his defense, hitting his arm, but again it just passed through the armor as if it were not there.

Herobrine stepped back and gave off a loud, maniacal laugh that caused the hundreds of zombies around him to also laugh and moan.

"Behold, the great User-that-is-not-a-user," Herobrine shouted to his troops. "You are about to witness the destruction of a legend. Watch closely my brothers as I take his life."

Herobrine scowled at Gameknight999 as his eyes glowed bright and menacing. The vile shadow-crafter looked about to make sure that his followers were watching, then charged at him with a speed that would have been thought impossible. And then the real battle began.

CHAPTER 27
SHAWNY

Moving at an impossible speed, Herobrine was suddenly behind Gameknight999, his ender sword slashing into Gameknight's armor. The shadowy blade tore a chunk away from his diamond coating. Spinning, the User-that-is-not-a-user brought up his sword to defend himself, but found that the shadow-crafter was already gone. Turning his head, he looked for his adversary, and found him standing a few blocks away, smiling an evil, devilish grin.

And then suddenly, the bright-eyed monster was on his side, his dark blade again wreaking havoc. Pain radiated through is body as the keen dark blade found flesh. Pushing Herobrine away with his free hand, Gameknight swung his blade in front of him to keep the shadow-crafter from advancing, but Herobrine had already disappeared. Turning, he looked to see where he would materialize, but then more pain erupted through his left arm as he felt the enderblade slash at his shoulder.

Rolling forward, Gameknight stood up and readied for the next attack. He had to figure out how to stop Herobrine; just standing here and letting his enemy cut him to pieces wasn't working. He also had the problem of all the zombies around him; if he was even able to defeat Herobrine, he'd still have to deal with all of them.

And then another piece of the puzzle clicked into place.

Moving slowly, Gameknight gradually shifted his position closer to the village. He'd take the battle closer to the walls.

Pain . . . Herobrine slashed at his legs, the dark blade making his armored leggings crack, another chunk of the protective diamond falling to the ground. Turning in a circle, Gameknight continued to move closer to the village walls, watching for his enemy's next appearance. Herobrine laughed in the distance, then appeared directly in front of him. Shoving him hard in the chest, the shadow-crafter knocked the User-that-is-not-a-user to the ground. As he landed with a thud, Gameknight started to panic.

What am I going to do? he thought. *I can't stop him . . . he's too fast . . . he's too strong.*

And then Herobrine was standing over him, stabbing downward with his dark sword. The shadowy blade struck his chest and formed another crack in the armor. Driving the blade down harder, the pointed tip found flesh and dug in. Yelling out in pain, Gameknight tried to roll away, but Herobrine had him pinned to the ground. He could feel his HP draining, getting dangerously low.

"You have no chance, User-that-is-not-a-user. Just take the Gateway of Light and you can live . . . or stay and die."

The dark blade came down again, this time piercing his shoulder. More pain shot through his body.

"You know you have to do it. All creatures want to live, even one as pathetic as you. Just use the Gateway and be safe . . . and then I'll be free."

He wants me to use the digitizer . . . why? He said he'll be free . . . free from what . . . from Minecraft . . . but why?

Herobrine disappeared, then reappeared a few blocks away. Scrambling to his feet, Gameknight backed away from the creature, moving closer to the city walls, the mass of zombies shifting with him.

"What is it you really want?" Gameknight asked as he shook his arm, trying to shake away the pain. "Tell me what it is that's going on here, and maybe I'll help you . . . that is . . . unless you are afraid to tell me."

"I fear NOTHING!" Herobrine spat. "Eventually you will take the Gateway of Light to escape your death and get out of Minecraft, and I'm going with you. You have no choice . . . it is inevitable."

"But you don't have a physical body to go to."

"You are so stupid . . . you think that all things are physical. I'm digital. I'm an artificially intelligent segment of code, and I want out of Minecraft. No longer will I be trapped within the confines of these puny servers. I will escape and I will have my revenge."

"He's a virus," Gameknight muttered, thinking out loud.

"What did you say?"

"I said you are the AI virus that has infected

Minecraft, aren't you?"

"Not a virus . . . living code . . . I am living code, and you have no idea what I am capable of doing once I escape Minecraft."

Herobrine disappeared and reappeared behind Gameknight999, slashing at his back. Another chunk of his diamond armor broke off and fell to the ground. Stabbing into the exposed flesh, Gameknight's body was overwhelmed with pain, waves and waves of pain. Swinging his blade, he caught Herobrine by surprise as his diamond sword sliced into the shadow-crafter, but again, his sword passed through his enemy as if he were made of air.

How am I going to defeat him? I can't touch him and he's too fast for me . . . I've lost.

And then suddenly a pop sounded next to Gameknight. Turning, he was surprised at what he saw: his friend Shawny standing there at his side, a big smile on his face, his server thread reaching high up into the air. Instantly, Gameknight could hear the villagers on the walls all drop their weapons and bring their arms together, linked across their chests. Herobrine, surprised by his appearance, teleported to five blocks away.

"Hi Gameknight . . . what's going on? Anything interesting happening?"

"Shawny . . . what are you doing here . . . how are . . . "

"Sorry friend . . . can't talk now. I have a demon to destroy."

Shawny then turned and faced Herobrine. His enchanted iron armor flickered as purple waves of magic flowed across the metallic coating.

"What is this?" Herobrine asked. "Who dares to interfere with my little game?"

Shawny said nothing and slowly walked toward

the shadow-crafter.

"You think I'm afraid of a *user?* I'll destroy you, then go back to playing with my little toy."

"We'll see," Shawny said as he put away his sword and brought out a bottle of some liquid.

"What are you doing? Pull out your sword and defend yourself," Herobrine said. "It's no fun destroying a helpless user. At least try to fight back."

Shawny said nothing, he just kept advancing, moving closer and closer to the monster. And when he was within 3 blocks, he threw the first bottle. The glass container flew through the air in a graceful arc, then landed at Herobrine's feet, breaking and splashing a blue liquid across the area. Some of the liquid splattered onto Herobrine's leggings. Instantly they started to smoke and sizzle.

Looking down at his legs, Herobrine was stunned at what was happening, a look of disbelief on his face. As he looked up, Shawny threw more bottles. The glass missiles struck him in the chest, causing his precious enderarmor to smoke as if on fire.

Sprinting toward his enemy, Shawny kept pummeling him with bottles, splashing more and more of the liquid across the enderarmor.

"What is this," Herobrine demanded, "some kind of poison?"

Shawny smiled as he threw more bottles at him.

"I thought the great Herobrine knew everything about Minecraft?" Gameknight said. The User-that-is-not-a-user had realized exactly what was in the bottles . . . the material that endermen fear the most. The bottles were filled with water; the liquid was deadly to endermen. And now it was damaging the enderarmor.

As Shawny ran around, throwing the water at Herobrine, Gameknight moved closer to the village walls. He could see the zombies move with him, keeping a respective distance from Herobrine and his prey. Glancing back at the shadow-crafter, he could see that the monster was now enveloped in smoke, the sizzling sound reminding Gameknight of frying bacon.

CRACK . . . one of the black armored plates cracked under the strain of the water.

"NOOOO!" Herobrine yelled and charged at the user.

Instead of drawing his sword, Shawny continued to throw bottles of water. When Herobrine reached him, his endersword slashed down upon the user, tearing a great gash in his iron armor. But Shawny, not *in* the game but just playing it, felt no pain.

Continuing to throw the bottles of water at the monster, Shawny sprinted away from Herobrine, trying to keep his distance while continuing to attack. A bottle splashed on the dark leggings . . . *CRACK* . . . then hit his boots . . . then splashed across his chest plate. The sizzling sound became louder as the water tore into the enderman flesh from which the armor was made.

Yelling out in frustration, Herobrine teleported away from his attacker and glared at him. He then slowly took off the dark armor, some of the pieces crumbling to the ground when they were removed, and stuffed them in his inventory. Sheathing his endersword, Herobrine drew his own diamond sword, then teleported back to Shawny and attacked. Slashing at him with great sweeping strokes, Herobrine quickly reduced his armor to nothing. Shawny drew his own enchanted diamond sword, but had little chance to defend himself as his attacker teleported from one place to the next, delivering lethal blows with each appearance.

In seconds, Shawny was gone, a pile of items

floating on the ground.

With his health partially revived, Gameknight turned away from this enemy and glanced up at his friends on the fortified wall. Waving his sword high in the air, he made sure that he had their attention, then turned to face his enemy.

"Hey, Herobrine," Gameknight shouted. "Let's finish what we started!"

He then pointed at the dark shadow-crafter with his shimmering sword. The evil creature looked back at Gameknight in disbelief, then a wry, malicious smile crept across his face. Noiselessly disappearing, Herobrine teleported to Gameknight's side, his sword already swinging. Anticipating this, Gameknight ducked as he slashed out at his enemy's legs. A glancing blow across his thigh made Herobrine step back, but just as quickly, he reappeared again, his sword swinging wildly. The diamond blade tore into Gameknight's chest, causing more pain, igniting every nerve. Herobrine then spun and swung at the nearly exposed legs, knocking the User-that-is-not-a-user to the ground. Gameknight tried to swing his sword at the monster standing over him, but a booted foot came down on his arm, pinning it to the ground.

"You are defeated," Herobrine said in a low voice, "and you are about to die. Your only chance is the Gateway of Light . . . take it and live."

"NEVER," Gameknight yelled. "I know you just want to escape from Minecraft, but I won't allow it. I refuse to unleash you on the physical world and I will never give up resisting you."

Herobrine laughed then pointed his sword at Gameknight999's chest. His eyes grew bright as a sneer spread across his terrible face.

"If you will not cooperate then you will die!"

As Herobrine raised his sword, Gameknight yelled out with all his strength.

"NOW, SHOOT THE TNT . . . SHOOT THE TNT!"

In an instant the air was filled with flaming arrows as every enchanted bow in the village fired at the red striped blocks of explosives. As soon as they hit the TNT, the flashing blocks fell down into the water, the embedded arrows sticking out like so many angry thorns. Herobrine stayed his attack and turned to look at the explosives, then looked at the deployment of his army. They were standing right next to the explosives, and when they went off it would be . . .

BOOM

BOOM . . . BOOM . . . BOOM

The landscape echoed with thunder as the TNT exploded, tearing a large crater in the ground where the blocks had stood. Looking across the landscape, Herobrine started to laugh.

"Your explosions did little damage," Herobrine said. "I have won!"

"Wait for it."

"What?"

"Wait for it . . . "

"What are you talking about?" Herobrine said as he glared down at Gameknight999.

"Look up."

Herobrine looked up, then suddenly teleported away. The sky was filled with the arrows that had been stuck into the blocks of TNT. Now thousands of arrows were just stopping their ascent and started falling to the ground, and the zombies were just standing there oblivious.

Dropping his sword, Gameknight pulled out his shovel and dug straight down, something only a noob to Minecraft would do, but right now he needed cover, fast. Digging down three blocks, Gameknight quickly placed a block of dirt above him and listened, trying to determine if his plan worked, or if death awaited him above.

CHAPTER 28
DIFFERENCES

In the darkness, he could hear the howling screams of pain as the cloud of arrows tore into the rotting green bodies. Digging up the block overhead, Gameknight climbed out of the hole and looked across the battlefield. Everywhere he saw wounded zombies, many popping out of existence as their HP diminished to zero. Confusion reigned across the rolling plains as injured zombies slowly climbed to their feet. Staring back across the field, Gameknight saw something colorful, a splash of bright yellow and red amidst the carnage and realized that it was that zombie girl that he'd seen standing with his sister; she was hurt. And as the zombies gradually realized what had happened, their dark hateful eyes slowly turned toward him.

Suddenly, a crash sounded as the village gates swung open and a huge collection of cavalry rode out, swords held up high. The horses' hooves sounded like thunder as they charged forward. The zombies, seeing this force, started to growl, their rage beginning to boil. The two great armies were about to clash, with Gameknight999 right in the middle.

"Attack them . . . attack!" Herobrine screamed

from a distant hill.

The shadow-crafter had teleported away just in time, escaping any harm: something that didn't go unnoticed by the zombie horde. With arrows sticking out of their green bodies, many of the zombies glared at the shadow-crafter with just as much anger as they had for the NPCs.

"STOP . . . WAIT!" a young voice yelled out.

Suddenly, the thunder stopped. Glancing toward the gates, he saw all the horses had halted their charge, the NPCs in their saddles looking uncertain. From the village gates strode a single zombie girl. She walked fearlessly across the battlefield with a confident stride, a look of anger on her face.

"THERE HAS BEEN ENOUGH KILLING . . . IT STOPS NOW!" the girl yelled to both NPCs and zombies.

Everyone was shocked by the ferocity of the girl's voice, and all were compelled to stay their hand and hold off with the fighting, at least for now.

She moved across the battlefield, ignoring the moaning of the zombies as if they were not there. When she reached Gameknight999 she stopped.

"What are you doing out here?" he asked.

"I'm going to stop this war and help my friend," she answered.

"What are you talking about?" he asked.

Monet pointed at the colorful heap on the ground.

"My friend . . . she's hurt," Monet answered.

Sprinting, she bolted toward Ba-Jin, Gameknight running close behind. As they neared the fallen zombie girl, Gameknight could see countless arrows sticking out through the colorful shirt; she was hurt . . . badly.

"Monet, she's probably going to die. You should just go back to the village and . . . "

"She's my friend and I'm going to help her," Monet

snapped. "You stay back."

"But I have to . . . "

Monet raised her hand and held it out straight, silencing her brother. She then turned and moved toward her friend. Kneeling on the ground, she slowly raised Ba-Jin and held her in her arms.

"Ba-Jin, it's me . . . Monet."

"Mo-Nay is alright?" the zombie asked.

"Yes, I am not harmed, but you look like you could use some help."

"Ba-Jin approaches death . . . this must be true. Great pain rages through this body and it is impossible to walk." Ba-Jin coughed, then moaned as she adjusted her position on the ground.

"But the other zombies, they can help you."

"That is not the zombie way. Zombies do not help other zombies, it does not serve the clan to help the weak."

"But not everything must serve the clan," Monet said.

"No, everything *must* . . . even Mo-Nay."

Monet closed her eyes for a moment as she reached out with her mind to Shawny. Then a bright green glow started to envelop both of them, the light seeming to come from Monet. As it grew brighter, Ba-Jin had to turn her head away and close her dark eyes to protect them from the emerald sun. But as the light slowly faded, Gameknight could see his sister in her user skin kneeling next to her zombie friend. She'd had Shawny turn off the zombie mod on her as well. Moving a step closer, he could hear the zombie gasp in surprise.

"A user . . . Mo-Nay is a user," Ba-Jin said.

"No . . . I'm not just a user. I'm your friend."

"Ba-Jin . . . I mean . . . *I* . . . don't have any friends."

"Well you do now, and this friend is going to help

you."

"But zombies don't help other . . . I mean, don't help . . . me."

"Ba-Jin, friends help out friends, no matter how different they may be on the outside," Monet said. "Now be quiet and rest."

Holding her tightly in her arms, Monet slowly rose to her feet and started walking toward another colorful zombie.

"Da-Ray, come help me!"

The red-shirted zombie just stood there, not knowing what to do.

"I said come here and help me with Ba-Jin!"

The zombie looked at the user, then glanced at the injured zombie in her arms.

"It's me, Monet, the one that painted that beautiful shirt that you now wear," Monet said. "You remember . . . sunsets . . . your favorite."

The zombie's eyes grew wide with surprise.

"Come here, Ba-Jin needs your help."

The monster took a hesitant step forward, then another and another until she was at Ba-Jin's side. Carefully, Monet put Ba-Jin into Da-Ray's arms, then looked down at the injured zombie.

"It will be alright, Ba-Jin," Monet said. "Da-Ray is going to get you back to the HP fountains, then maybe both of you can help some of these others."

Da-Ray looked around at the battlefield. She could see numerous zombies that lay on the ground, many near death. She then looked back at Monet and nodded.

"We . . . I mean . . . *WE* will help the others," Da-Ray said.

Turning her head, Da-Ray looked back at some of the other multicolored zombies and motioned each to come help. The decorated monsters all moved forward and sped past them, running to the fallen that struggled to stand. Each took a zombie and helped them to their feet. Then other zombies, those that were not colored by Monet, also stepped forward and helped their friends to their feet. With green decaying arms around the wounded, they headed back toward zombie-town and the life-giving HP fountains.

Da-Ray started to turn and follow the other zombies, but Ba-Jin reached out and grabbed Monet's sleeve.

"Wait," the zombie moaned.

Da-Ray stopped and turned back to Monet.

Moving closer, Monet113 looked down at her friend and gently stroked her square cheeks.

"I shall miss you, Mo-Nay," Ba-Jin said in a hoarse voice.

"No, *we* shall miss you," Da-Ray added.

Ba-Jin nodded.

"You have taught us something wonderful," Ba-Jin continued. "People that are different can also be the same . . . inside."

Now it was Monet that nodded, a tear rolling down her square face.

"Go, Da-Ray, before it is too late," Monet said. "Get her to the fountains and pass on what you have learned to the others."

"We will," both zombies said, then smiled to each other.

Turning, Da-Ray shuffled away, her precious cargo held carefully in her green arms. As she passed one of the adult zombies, the creature stepped forward and surveyed the battlefield. A look of sadness came across the creature's green scarred face, then he held his hand up high, claws extended, then shouted in a loud, scratchy voice.

"To those that died for the clan, the salute of

sacrifice is given."

Many of the zombies heading out onto the battlefield stopped and turned toward the lone voice, then also held up their spiked hands, claws gleaming in the moonlight. They leaned their heads back and howled a sorrowful moan that was filled with such a sadness that many of the NPCs wept upon hearing it, Gameknight and Monet included.

"For the good of the clan," a zombie shouted.

"For the good of the . . . " shouted another, but didn't finish the statement.

"For the good . . . " The statement was incomplete.

"For the . . . " The zombie couldn't continue as they stood witness to the carnage that sat before them.

The zombies stopped the recitation and just held up their clawed hands, heads held back in sadness for those that had died, then lowered their hands and moved toward those that needed help. Looking over his shoulder, Gameknight could see looks of surprise on the NPCs that viewed the scene. They'd seen the zombies give the salute for the dead, a similar salute the NPCs used, and many realized that maybe there *was* something in common with the green creatures.

Looking back across the battle, Gameknight smiled as he watched the zombies help up their comrades . . . friends for the first time helping friends. And instead of a wave of hate crashing down upon the village, the massive army of zombies was just walking away, the burden of their anger and prejudice for the moment set aside so that they could shoulder the responsibility of helping those in need.

In the distance, he could hear Herobrine screaming out in frustration.

"What are you doing . . . ATTACK!" the shadow-crafter yelled, but the zombies ignored the violent cries and focused on helping their comrades, now friends for the first time. "Noooo!"

Then Herobrine turned his attention toward Gameknight999. The User-that-is-not-a-user could feel the hateful glare focus down on him, his eyes glowing bright.

"You have ruined everything! I'm going to . . . "

Suddenly, the forest was filled with the howls of animals. Looking to the tree line, Gameknight could see pairs of eyes appear in the shadows, their eyes burning a bright red as they stared toward Herobrine. Slowly the eyes moved out of the forest, and a pack of a hundred wolves moved out into the clearing, all of them heading for Herobrine. Gameknight could see their fur bristling with tension and anger, all focused on the shadow-crafter.

Turning to look at the vile creature, Gameknight could see that Herobrine actually looked afraid, as if he knew that these animals were after him. Disappearing noiselessly, Herobrine appeared on a distant hill. He pointed toward Gameknight999 with his diamond sword, then yelled at the top of his voice.

"THIS ISN'T OVER, USER-THAT-IS-NOT-A-USER. YOU *WILL* DO AS I COMMAND AND RELEASE ME FROM THIS PRISON . . . OR YOU WILL DIE."

Hearing the voice in the distance, the wolves all howled, then sprinted directly for the dark shadow-crafter, their growls filling the air. Seeing their advance, Herobrine snarled one last time toward Gameknight999, then disappeared.

The wolves, sensing their prey had gone, turned and headed back into the forest, leaving Gameknight999 and Monet113 alone on the battlefield. Sprinting, Gameknight moved to her side.

"Come, we have to get back to the village," Gameknight said.

Monet nodded and turned, heading back toward

the gates.

"Was Shawny able to get the digitizer working?" she asked.

He shook his head.

"He thinks that we need Dad to fix it, but he's still gone on his business trip," Gameknight999 replied, then his voice grew angry. "Why can't he be home, just this once? I miss him."

Monet113 said nothing, just looked at the ground as they walked, then brought her brightly colored head up and looked at her brother.

"Me too, but Mom says that he's doing what he needs to do to support us," she said.

"Being away doesn't seem like a very good way to support a family," Gameknight snapped. "But come on, let's get back to the others."

They ran back to the village, and as they passed through the gates, the NPCs erupted in cheers, everyone chanting for the User-that-is-not-a-user and the Sister-of-Gameknight999.

CHAPTER 29
LEGEND OF THE ORACLE

Quickly, we can attack them before they get away," Hunter said.

"No, let them go," Gameknight999 said in a stern voice.

"But they're zombies, and they'll be back," she replied.

"Maybe," Crafter added as he moved his horse forward to the front of the cavalry, "but today it will be live and let live. Maybe this will help the relationship between NPCs and zombies . . . somehow."

"LIVE AND LET LIVE?" Hunter screamed. "What are you talking about . . . they're zombies . . . they aren't friends."

"Not yet . . . but I have hope," Monet said. "We've seen the beginning of something today, the smallest ripple of change within the zombies of zombie-town, and we don't know how this ripple will grow."

"Ripple . . . change . . . we're talking about zombies!" Hunter continued. "We have nothing in common with them. They are monsters and we are NPCs."

"They did the salute to the dead," one of the villagers said from the crowd that had now gathered at the gates.

"And they looked sad over those that they lost . . . maybe they have feelings," another added.

Hunter looked at them all, a look of frustration on her face, and was about to say something until Crafter settled his small hand on her shoulder.

"We can debate this later . . . right now, we need a plan," the young NPC said.

Gameknight turned and looked across the battlefield. He could see the last remnants of the zombie army slowly trudging their way into the forest, monsters with their green arms wrapped around the wounded, helping each other for the first time. Looking at the creatures, he could see there was something different about them. They did not have the normal angry look to their eyes; they were not snarling or growling . . . the creatures were just walking away.

Suddenly, he noticed someone at his side. Turning, he found Stitcher standing next to him. She wrapped her arms around him and gave him a warm hug.

"I'm glad you're OK," she said.

"I'm pretty happy about that too," he replied. "But I have to tell you, Herobrine had me pretty scared. I don't know if he can be defeated in battle." He paused to look at the faces of his comrades, their worried gazes focused on him. "I'm sure he'll be back for me, but next time it will be with more monsters."

Crafter turned and faced the User-that-is-not-a-user. "We will be more prepared next time," the young NPC said, his voice ringing with wisdom.

"How?" Gameknight snapped. "You saw all the zombies that were coming out of those tunnels in the zombie-town. I'm sure there are hundreds of zombie-towns on this server, and all of them will be sending monsters here . . . for me. He also said something about the Sisters, whatever that meant, but I bet it's not a good thing. We have to do something."

Gameknight stopped talking and waited to hear ideas from his friends, but all he heard was silence. Nobody knew what to do, but as he looked in all their faces he could see the fear that was present deep in their eyes.

This village won't survive if I stay here, he thought. *I have to do something to protect these people.*

Suddenly, two young NPCs ran up to him, each one wrapping their arms around a leg. Looking down, he could see that it was Topper and Filler, Digger's twin boys.

"Careful," Digger said as he walked out of the village gates and moved near Gameknight. "His armor is cracked in many places, you kids don't want to get cut or hurt."

He looked down at his diamond armor and could see huge cracks. In some places, there were chunks of armor missing: remnants of the endersword's sting. Reaching down, Gameknight gently pulled the two children back and knelt.

"We're glad you're OK, Gameknight," Topper said.

"Yeah, we were scared," Filler added.

"So was I, kids, but now everything is OK."

Gameknight looked at Digger and could see the worried parental look on his face. This was a father concerned for his children, and he knew that the User-that-is-not-a-user was the source of the danger.

And Gameknight agreed.

If he stayed here, then he would put them all in danger. When Shawny was able to get the digitizer working again, then he could get out of Minecraft, but . . . but then Gameknight remembered Herobrine's words: *Eventually you will take the Gateway of Light . . . and I'm going with you.* He realized that it didn't matter if Shawny got the digitizer to work. As soon as Gameknight tried to escape the game, Herobrine could teleport next to him and escape with him. Gameknight999 could not let that happen. There was no choice but to destroy Herobrine before he and Monet had any shot at going back to the real world . . . they'd have to destroy him first, somehow.

But how?

Uncertainty surged through Gameknight. He had to do something to protect these NPCs . . . they were like his family in Minecraft and he couldn't endanger them. He also had to protect his sister. But he knew that if he stayed here, then Herobrine would be back.

Clasping his hands behind his back, he walked out of the village gates and across the battlefield, thinking. As he moved away from the village one of the puzzle pieces fell into place . . . and then another and another fell into order until he could see the entire solution to the problem.

We have to go away!

Turning, he faced his friends.

"I know what to do," he said, his voice firm. "I have to go away until my friends in the physical world can fix the Gateway of Light. Then I'll have to face Herobrine and defeat him somehow before going home again. But I can't stay here; I'll be putting you all in danger."

He looked down at Topper and Filler, then up to Digger.

"I won't risk any of your lives, and certainly not my sister's . . . this is between Herobrine and me."

Crafter started to object but Gameknight cut him off.

"NO! It's decided, and it starts now. And don't try to say you should come with me. I won't have any warriors risking their lives for me and that's final. I'm going to go out into the wild and hide while those in the physical world get the Gateway of Light working again."

"Well I'm going with you," Monet said.

"You can't," Gameknight told his sister. "It's too dangerous facing Herobrine, and I won't risk losing you. You're my responsibility in here."

"*Your* responsibility? I saved your butt back there

by convincing all of the zombies not to fight," Monet said.

Gameknight didn't know what to say. He hadn't thought of it like that.

"Your sister is right," Crafter said. "We all would have died if it wasn't for Monet. She saved us all."

"The way I see it," Monet added, "making sure nothing bad happens to you is *my* responsibility. 'Family takes care of family'. . . right?"

Gameknight looked at his sister, realizing that he was very proud of her, proud of how brave she was in standing up to Xa-Tul and for convincing the zombies not to stay and fight. She was right, he realized, he might need her help after all.

"Alright," he said, with a grin on his face. "I guess I could use a traveling partner."

Monet smiled.

"Besides, I'm kinda getting used to having you in Minecraft with me," Gameknight added. "Don't tell anyone, because I'll deny that I said it, but I like having you in here with me."

She smiled even bigger, then wrapped her arms around him and gave him a big hug. He hugged her back, then let go and turned to face the village.

"Farewell my friends, we will return after Herobrine has been defeated and we've used the Gateway of Light to get home again. Goodbye."

Without waiting for anyone to respond, he turned and started walking away from the village, his sister at his side. Drawing his sword, he headed for the forest. He knew that this would be like hardcore Minecraft, but worse. As he walked, Gameknight thought about what he'd need to do: get resources, make a hidey-hole, find food . . . all that things that you normally did in Minecraft. Only this time it would be to save his life, and possibly the whole world as well.

Lost in thought, he didn't notice the small NPC that fell in next to him, walking lock-step with him. When he realized it, he looked down and found Topper walking next to him.

"You said you wouldn't have any warriors risking their lives for you," Topper said. "Well, I'm not a warrior, Gameknight999. I'm a topper. I put the tops on bottles. You didn't say anything about toppers not being allowed to go with you."

"And I'm not warrior, I'm a filler," Filler said on his left. "You didn't say anything about fillers either."

Gameknight stopped and looked down at the boys, overcome with emotion.

"I didn't hear anything about diggers either," a deep voice said behind him.

Turning, he found Digger standing behind him, his iron pickaxe on his shoulder. Behind him was the entire village . . . men, women, and children all filing out of the gates to follow the User-that-is-not-a-user.

"Nothing about bakers . . . " one voice said.

"Or carvers . . . "

"Or weavers . . . "

"Or grinders . . . "

"Or . . . " The litany went on and on as the NPCs stated their intentions to go with their friend, their hero, into the unknown.

And as the villagers filled out of their town, Crafter came up next to him.

"We are all with you, User-that-is-not-a-user," the young NPC said, his voice, as always, ringing with aged wisdom. "Family takes care of family, and you and your sister are a part of our village's family."

"Family takes care of family?" Gameknight asked.

Crafter nodded. "Do you have any plan at all?" he

asked in a low voice.

Gameknight looked down at him and said nothing.

"I thought so," the young NPC replied. "Well, if you have no ideas at all, then maybe I could suggest one."

"What?"

"My Great Aunt Milky once told me of a story she heard when she was young."

"I'm listening."

"She said that there is an ancient temple in the jungle. It is the oldest temple in Minecraft."

Click . . . one of the puzzle pieces fell into place.

"And in that temple lives the oldest being in Minecraft. She is called the Oracle."

"The Oracle?" Gameknight999 and Monet113 asked in unison.

Click . . . another piece found its home.

"Yes, she is the oldest NPC in Minecraft, and she knows things that nobody else knows about how everything works. Milky said that some claimed the Oracle is actually not an NPC at all, but something different . . . something more . . . something that was added to Minecraft to keep everyone safe. Maybe she can help."

"Do you know where to find this Oracle?"

"I have some ideas," Crafter answered.

Click . . . click . . . click . . . more pieces fell into place, but there were still many parts of the puzzle that remained a mystery.

"Then that's as good a place as any . . . lead on."

Crafter turned and moved back to his horse and climbed up, then brought a horse for Gameknight999.

"No thanks, I'll walk," he said. "If there isn't enough for everyone, then I'll just stay down here. Besides," he sheathed his sword then reached down and grabbed the hand of Topper while Monet grabbed Filler's, "I have these two to protect us . . . right?"

"Right," echoed Monet.

"Alright then," Crafter said, then turned in his saddle and shouted to the rest of the NPCs. "Follow me to the jungle temple Oracle."

"This sounds like another one of your great ideas, Gameknight," Hunter said with a smile, then kicked her horse and rode off to scout ahead, Stitcher falling in with her older sister.

Looking behind, Gameknight999 was touched by the devotion these people had for him and his sister, not because he was Gameknight and she was Monet, or because he was the User-that-is-not-a-user, but because they were part of their family . . . and family always takes care of family . . . even younger sisters.

Smiling, he turned and walked toward the mystical Oracle that was out there, somewhere, he and his sister holding the hands of the twins and enjoying the sweet music of Minecraft.